WHAT I DID FOR LOVE

MICKEY J CORRIGAN

BLOODHOUND
— BOOKS —

Print ISBN : 978-1-913419-14-1

PART I

THE FALL

1

Mojito, the drink of my choice. My heart and my reason, my loss of reason. So wrong for me. But now, without Mojito, my life is an empty glass.

Mojito is not his real name, of course. It is the pseudonym I will use while I tell you this story. To protect his reputation. He was not of age.

Gasp. You are horrified? Well, that is my point, you see. To draw you in with the tawdry steam of my situation, my obsession, my bad choices.

What I mean to say is, picture this: under a gaudy blue sky, a tanned young man in colorful board shorts lopes across the hot white sand to the turquoise Florida surf. A tall golden lightly muscled teenager, fully emerged from boyhood, but not yet a hardened man. Imagine watching him toss the shiny yellow board into the clutch of the aqua waves and jump on. He lays flat, paddles out. Deftly shaking the sea from his eyes and hair. Wet, joyful, like a young seal. So carefree, strong, full of spirit. Full of life.

Got that? Now, imagine this: a middle-aged woman standing alone on the tideline, staring at the distant horizon. Thirsty, licking at her sun-dried lips. Wearing a broad-brimmed hat to shade her fine skin. Her freckles. Her (dear God) wrinkles.

You see now?

Was he the first young man I lusted after? No. I'd wanted others before him. So he had a precursor? He did, of course. I've loved many men over the years, men younger than I. In fact, I always preferred my men unseasoned. Even as a high school junior and senior, I liked the middle school boys with their wide eyes and virginal smiles. I kicked my cheerleader legs high for those kids seated passively in the stadium. I lured them in, the ripening jocks. By their freshman year, many of them had already been mine.

And in college? I did not respond to the creative writing professor who called me to his weed-hazy office in order to ogle my model figure and make suggestive comments on my work. No, thank you. Unlike the other coeds, I did not worship the ice hockey studs with their bearish manes and campus swagger. Instead, I had my heart set on the genius kid. You know, the four-eyed geek who skipped high school to breeze through college on a three-year track. I wanted his black-framed glasses on the floor beside my futon. I wanted his serious little face pressed against my naked skin.

That's how it's always been for me. Give me the boys, burning young and bright. Hold me up to these hot new suns and bake me to a crisp. After, I will cover myself with coconut crème and soak in tequila and lime.

But this Mojito, he was nothing but a typical American surf rat, you say? Not true. When the ride was high, he slipped away to test and retest his body and his prowess. Yes, he did. But he worked hard between wave sessions. High school senior by day, plus community college classes at night, studying on weekends for the SATs. He wasn't slacking. Too energetic for that, too full of plans for his blazing future.

My mouth is so dry. It needs wetting. The drink I crave, however, is not available. Will never be available again.

Back then in that dream, I slaked myself as often as possible. I lived high above the unfurling sea in a castle on the sugary sand, he in his father's princedom on the peaceful Intracoastal Waterway. I know, my prose here is laughable. But you can always count on a seductive murderess to have a book in her. We always do, you see.

So, ladies and gentlemen of the jury, please take a hard look at exhibit A. Mojito, there in the distance on his colorful surf-board, glorious in the glance of the afternoon sun. The salt water glistening on his hairless chest. Toothpaste smile gleaming against the blue green water. Honey blond hair long as a girl's, but prettier. Wet trunks clinging to seaside thighs.

And me, here at the defense table. Pale, withering. Juiceless. Dry, so very dry.

He was a child, you say? Ha. He was *seventeen*. Smart. Aware. Sexy. Jacked on testosterone, full of passion. He had so much to look forward to. He was beauty. He was youth. Energy. Vitality. Everything that is irresistible to old age.

And me? I was incapable of resisting his youth-soaked charms. Because there *I* was, looking ahead to what? To growing only older. My lord, I was gripped by a funhouse mirror. I saw myself warped, in crisis, tumbling ever faster down the bumpy hill from forty. A woman alone, trying to survive the avalanche of aging, buried alive in unquenched desire.

On that, you see, I rest my case.

My story is, of course, a tangle of roses, stones, and broken glass. Someone had to bleed.

2

"If he doesn't turn in the paper by Monday, I will have to give him an incomplete for the term," I told Mojito's father, a tall graying man with a sincere handshake and a shy smile. "And I don't want to do that. He could do so well if he took the time to focus on this class."

I always said that kind of thing to the concerned parents. Usually, it was bunk. But in this case, it was largely true. Mojito was not like most of my students. They tended to be disinterested kids of average intelligence with zero motivation to tap what they'd been given. Mojito was different. Capable, ambitious, and from what I could see in class, highly intelligent. But he was focusing on his college classes to such an extent that he no longer took high school seriously. Even though he needed the grades to get into a top university. Not the local college where he studied part-time. No, he deserved much better than that, which is what I told his father that day.

"This sometimes happens with dual-enrolled students," I said, removing my reading glasses to look at the man. He had nice eyes. Charcoal gray but with a tinge of blue, almost perfectly matching his sharply cut Armani suit.

Mr. Mojito nodded, his handsome face serious. "I understand, Ms. O'Hale. I will make this quite clear to him tonight at dinner." He began to rise from the metal chair, then sat again with a sigh. He looked at me across my cluttered desk. His eyes were like a wolf's, but lacked guile. I thought he might be a good man. "His mother left us when Mojito was only six. I have done my best but I can only pray he doesn't go off-track."

The way he was looking at me indicated his mind was not on his son's immediate future but, instead, his own.

He cleared his throat. I thought, here it comes. The *why don't we continue this discussion over a nice bottle of wine?*

I stiffened. Yes, he was attractive. And he dressed like he had class, and plenty of money. But I would never date the parent of one of my students. One of my students, maybe. But not the old man.

He caught my eyes and scooped them up, his smile so sweet it was unnerving. "I was wondering..."

They are always wondering, these mature self-confident men. Wondering what it would take to seduce their kid's teacher. The old maid who existed only for her students. A creature of negative space who lived alone, drank tea with lemon, and pet her slinky cat while marking up homework papers in red ink.

"Would you join us for dinner one night? We would love to have you to the house. Mojito speaks highly of you. He tells me you have read all the classics. I too love literature."

Yeah, right. All the old guys said this over the first drink. Then it turned out they had never heard of Zora Neale Hurston. Marguerite Duras. Lucia Berlin. The great *female* writers. I could understand the kids' ignorance. But I did not make excuses for the grown men who did not have enough curiosity to seek out truly great literature.

When I shook my head, Mr. Mojito reached over to put a

hand on mine. His skin was cool, pampered, soft. Yes, he was definitely wealthy. This was not a man who held hammers, crowbars, tire irons, dead fish. His manicure was nicer than mine.

"Please. Think about my offer. You don't have to answer, not now. This is a standing invitation. In the meantime, I will see to it that my son does his homework for Monday. Perhaps then you will agree to come to our house."

Not likely. Not unless the father was away on business and Mojito and I could...

An image of the boy flashed in my mind like a strobe. The first time I saw him outside class, jogging down the beach. His tanned back, smooth and rippling with new muscles. His long, wet hair. The tight ass.

Swiftly, I stood, pulling my hand away. Then I thanked Mr. Mojito for meeting with me to discuss my concerns about his son's schoolwork.

And so it began. The beginning of everything, the end of everything. How poetic. How unexpected for someone of my invisible status. For so long I was nobody. Now I am everybody's nightmare.

Where did I come from and how did I arrive at this point, you wonder. I wish I could say I was born in Paris and lived a glamorous life, but that would be a lie. I prefer not to lie to you now. The truth is, my life was unglamorous. In fact, it was dull. So dull it was almost normal. Like a glass of clear liquor with just a twist of lemon.

Sex being the twist.

Perhaps I should have seen a shrink. Taken anti-something-or-other medications. Detoxed, twelve-stepped, converted to Zen. Perhaps I might have averted disaster. But then there would have been no story to share, no book. No great doomed love.

There's no psychic reason to explain my predilection. I had

an unremarkable childhood. A certain amount of family largesse and privilege, with too little affection. I would not pin *all* the blame there. That's a cop out. But lacking the flattering touch I desired, I naturally sought attention from the opposite sex. When my younger brother brought his friends home from grade school, I taught them silly games we could play in the dark corners of the cellar. Later, Hugh brought home his prep school roommates, gangly boys with crackling voices and hands that needed guidance.

I developed a reputation, and I was proud of it. Mrs. Robinson, the boys called me. Ha ha.

I won't tell you how old I was when I lost my virginity. And you do not want to hear how my sweet partner cried afterward. He was afraid of what his mother would say. That is until I told him not to tell her. He brightened then, and we did it a second time. I loved being able to comfort and advise, as inexperienced as I was. Me, taking control. Such a heady feeling.

High school, college, and always the younger boys milling about. Sweet kids who were ready, willing, always able and able and able. Times were fast, adventurous, exciting. And I was in charge. The boys, they were unconscious of their fantastic power. And therefore, did not abuse it.

While working toward my PhD in English literature, however, I reined in my appetites. Determined to stay focused, I avoided the temptation of high-riding testosterone in favor of nose to the grindstone. I practiced sexual discipline, reassuring myself that I could do so. That I would thus avoid making mistakes once I was ensconced in a teaching position. That is, if I chose to.

The key word being *chose*.

Graduate school served as a period of intense celibacy. I had something to prove to myself and I did just that. I practiced the art of resistance for five long years. I tried to be good, I really did.

No sense being a professor, then losing out on tenure due to indiscretion. I learned to swallow my raging thirsts in favor of mature responsibility and a life of the mind. I embraced adulthood.

Or so I convinced myself.

By the time I graduated, I had lowered the bar on my career expectations. Why kill myself, and for what? I decided I was only interested in teaching the least rigorous of coursework. Florida Beach University accepted my application for a part-time lecturer position, and I moved to the east coast of the sunshine state.

I stayed away from family. My parents' bickering had become intolerable. I'd watched their petty differences change them from intelligent people into clawing animals. They remained on the west coast of Florida, where many of my relatives lived, and I kept the Everglades between us. I stayed single, refusing to embark on long-term relationships with the lineup of age-appropriate suitors who seemed interested in more than my body. Which, as I think I have already intimated, was sizzling hot.

I wanted to ignore the rest of them too, all the men who wished only to have sex with me. I tried to dress down, quelling my ardor, or they would flock, bloodripe, and I would be forced to confront them, to say no or to give in and have sex. And I was no good at resistance. I have a weakness, you see, one that I cannot overcome.

Obviously.

So my choice of relocation was purposeful. I was hidden away in the humid swamps of a forgotten town, teaching in a bottom-tier college. In sleepy Stormy Beach, I was no longer prey on crowded streets swarming with horny stalkers and pheromone sniffers. I was not exposed to daily temptation, and the living was easy. In Stormy Beach, I thought I was safe from them, and from my own desires.

Ha.

Determined to make the quiet little beach town my permanent home, I qualified for a mortgage on a one-bedroom condo overlooking the inlet. After teaching intro English lit and creative writing classes to dimwits all day, I spent long nights in the blue glare of my laptop, either out on my balcony or down by the condominium pool. I sat cross-legged on lounge chairs in the semidarkness that washed softly over the starlit water, working on a short story.

Then another. And another.

All were unpublished. Rejected again and again by the elitist literary presses. Each letter of refusal had the rich flavor of hell. It infuriated me, the editors' blindness to my creative genius. They preferred the silly to the serious, publishing only the fake fiction by the popular frauds.

Fortunately, due to my current life circumstances, this kind of homicidal dismissal will not be the sad fate that greets the story I am working on now. The one you are reading with such avid and perverse interest. I can just imagine it: the slight spittle forming on your lips, the lurid glare in your dark circled eyes. But listen, please. I did not plan on things turning out this way. This was not the plot I had in mind. However, I do take comfort in the turn of events. It bodes well for my literary aspirations.

A casual day-to-day routine firmly established in Stormy Beach, I kept to myself and avoided romance. At work, I dutifully lectured dullards more interested in their phone screens than the shocking beauty of works by Nabokov, Nïn, D.H. Lawrence. After work, I drove home and ran the beach. Shower, salad, writing until midnight. That was it. My life. Could it get any drier?

No. Which explains why I started drinking. Light beer at

first, but one turned into six, my thirst never quite quelled. After dabbling in white wines, I branched out to the reds. Cardbordeaux. Soon enough I moved on to shots of tequila. Bottles of Mexican tequila. The hard stuff.

Needless to say, my commitment to celibacy evaporated and blew away in the briny wind. I traded running for happy hours, writing at night for sex on the sand. But none of my partners were appropriate. Always immature. Not ready for commitment. Not ready for adult life.

I am not talking about kids here. I am referring to grown men. This is who I picked up in the beach bars. Twenty-five, thirty, even at thirty-nine years old, these men were still boys. Apparently, while I had been growing older, the boys had all *stayed* boys. They seemed to have been, somehow, retarded in their maturation processes. They only *looked* older. Balding, spare tired, their teeth yellowed. They looked too old for me, in fact. But there was no debate: they were all boys. Groping, silly, cloddish. Needy. Overly chummy and sexually selfish. Many of them lived at home. *Never grow up* was apparently their unspoken vow. Where, I wondered, was Peter Pan?

When I had sex with these unappealing strangers, I wished I was home writing. Or slitting my wrists. Because I could not feel anything. I thought that part of me had died.

I kept drinking, but stopped going out with men. I preferred my lovers younger. Much younger, and willing to grow. Unschooled and looking to me for life lessons. How to please a woman. In the bedroom, in the kitchen, in every room. How to set a table for a woman, pull out her chair. Which fork, which wine. Yes, do apply to the MBA program, your salary will take a sweet jump. No, do not ask out your best friend's girl. Even though she's *super hot*. Wait until she wants you. Win her over, then let her come to you. Be a little hipper, a little cooler than your friend is. Than anyone else is.

A decade passed in this way. I drank, had occasional sex with a younger guy not quite young enough to please me, and went to work every day. I was always discreet around my job. There I remained the cool lit prof, sober, serious, but exuding something. The sexy-librarian teacher, the one the bad boys liked to wonder about. I was mysterious, aloof, tempting but unapproachable.

By then I had to wear reading glasses. And I would make discreet visits to the local anti-aging clinic for lipo or Botox. Things were beginning to fall apart. I needed a thumb in that dike hole. But whose?

Of course, I remained single. The older guys I had fooled around with, they were never an option. And how could I marry a deliciously younger man when it was obvious I was their superior? Their boss. Their font of womanly knowledge. The oil in their shiny new engines. I made things run. Then they drove away.

Not that I wanted them to stay. Just that most women my age had been married. At least once, sometimes twice. If you are a woman over forty and have no ring, no children, then who are you in this society? Unless you are the CEO of a Fortune 500 company, you are nobody. You are alone.

I had my career, at least. When the opportunity arose, I left FBU for a cushy job at Caligula High. My days were shorter, the summers did not entail a minute of classwork, and my students were rippling with young energy. Cute boys drove in from the three contiguous beach towns. Not smart enough for private schools with International Baccalaureate programs, these were the regular kids with team sports, girlfriends, bros they hung with. After-school video game marathons in their parents' rec rooms. Surfboards and dirt bikes. Long hair.

Yum.

Some saw through my reserved teacher veneer to my sex and

my soul. They bristled when I walked by, inhaling my natural perfume, marveling at my wisdom and maturity. They looked deep in my eyes when I scanned the class, tried to hold my glance, convey their need.

Maybe I reminded them of Mom. Or Mom's best friend. The one hot friend boys always lust after. Secretly.

The key word being *secretly*.

Now, please understand I did wish to keep my job. So I was discreet. That first year at Caligula, I drank less and only at night. I was well behaved, nearly celibate, but then I got thirsty again. Still, I was careful. I was always so careful. Until the affair with Mojito exploded in my face, I believed my sexual history was private. I certainly never spoke of it. Who would I tell?

When I first moved to Stormy Beach, I looked much younger than my age. The sun, the dry spells, the drinking, all of that has not been kind to me. But at Caligula, I still had it going on. The boys stuck around after class. They sent me texts. Not sexts, mind you. I am not stupid. No, they would send me long sad stories about their dreamy ambitions, their pathetic longings, their broken families. What was I, their counselor? Their substitute mother? No. But I *was* kind. Boys deserve kindness. I know boys. They seem shallow but are actually so very deep. And helpless. They think they must wait for you to feed them like baby birds, small mouths open to receive.

On occasion, I fed them. Just a few select baby birds were rewarded with my special care and attention.

Now that my fate has uncovered my softest belly, exposing my utmost vulnerability to the world, they have come back to peck at me. Or so it seems. They all speak of me publicly now. Of the horrible things I did. What crimes I committed! Apparently, making a young man's sexual fantasies come true is a terrible thing. I victimized them, trampling on their innocent trust of adults.

According to current state statutes, if I were aged twenty-three or younger, having sex with a minor of sixteen or seventeen would not be punishable by the courts. But since I was older than that and my willing partner under the age of eighteen? Well then, my intent was criminal. Not sexual, but unlawful. And perverse.

Okay, so I had younger lovers, yes. Does this make me a criminal? I think not. Murder, well, yes, that *was* a crime. For that, I must take responsibility. But not the sex. I may have been forty-plus, Mojito not yet eighteen. But it was consensual, our love. One hundred percent mutual.

When I tell you the story, you will have to agree. In fact, you will view my story with impartial sympathy. Because you will understand the truth of the situation. How he wanted it even more than I did. I am a teacher, after all. What I was doing with Mojito, in school and out, was my job.

That my job is my passion is, I think, a blessing. And, apparently, also a curse.

3

When I pulled off A1A at the address Mr. Mojito had provided, I halted before a towering front gate of rich cherry-colored wood. I had to press a buzzer and speak to the housekeeper or someone deep inside the estate. Announce myself as a guest of the Mojito family. Extremely wealthy, is what I was thinking as I said, "Dr. O'Hale to see Mr. Mojito and son. For lunch."

Whoever it was opened the gate for me. I waited as the heavy door slid back to reveal a thick green jungle overhanging a narrow drive consisting of small multi-colored stones. My Volvo crunched across the polished gravel rocks, sliding between swathes of fuchsia bougainvillea, clumps of spiky saw palmettos and mother-in-law tongues, towering and majestic royal palms. Black-hooded parrots squawked overhead. Crickets chirruped.

After several friendly phone calls and a flurry of E-mail invitations, I had finally agreed to visit. But not for dinner. No, only for lunch by the pool. Casual, out in the open. I had been quite sure I could handle it. Be professional. Possibly enjoy myself.

But now I was nervous, trembling slightly. The house was a white cement monolith with tinted green glass. It was set high on the lot like a decorated cake on a stand. A convertible Rolls was parked in the circular drive. I imagined there had to be a gleaming yacht in the backyard, anchored in the Intracoastal and ready to head off to the Caribbean. Maybe a helicopter landing pad somewhere. Tennis courts. An Olympic-size infinity pool.

I grew up with money, but not like this. Seeing the extravagant expanse before me, all that garish excess, made my shaking hands even more unsteady.

What I needed was a drink.

Fortunately, I was not traveling naked. I took a boozy hit from my insulated coffee thermos that doubled as a flask, then tucked it back in the cup holder. After I parked the car under a massive sea grape tree, I popped a breath mint and climbed out. It was a beautiful autumn day, the sun high overhead and bright, but not piercing like it is in the summer months. The breeze off the water was cooling and sweet.

I was glad I had worn low heels because the stone drive would have been tricky in stilettos and the three marble steps were steep and slick. As I reached the landing, the tall double doors opened before me. And there he was. Mojito.

Mo-hee-toe.

A neon green T-shirt, tight and tucked into worn jeans. His lithe frame was filling out nicely, his five o'clock shadow a reddish gold. And those beautiful eyes. Oh God, oh God.

He smiled at me, flashing bright white teeth. I smiled in return. My heart? *Rat-a-tat. Ratatatat!*

Why was this happening to me? And why now? I was always so cool in class. But here I was on his exclusive turf and, in that sense, he was in control. My legs weakened, like they were made of pudding. I stood there on the top step, unmoving, silent. I stood there staring at him like a fool.

"Good to see you, Dr. O."

That's what the students called me, *Dr. O*. Their parents eliminated the appellation and referred to me as Miz O'Hale. Maybe this made them feel less intimidated. I didn't care either way.

But when Mojito said my name, my heart skipped rope. Quickly, happily, like a giddy child.

Standing before him, I only came up to his chin. Maybe the heels would have been a good idea after all. He smiled down at me, as if he were the teacher and I the bumbling student. As if he were the brilliant young doctor who would cure all my aches. He was like a rock star onstage, his pulsating energy, the tumultuous music I heard when I looked at him, all of that moved me. He somehow struck with gentle force the most sensitive chord in my heart. And my loins.

Exhibit B, people: he was aware, but not conniving. He did not seduce me, but initiated my seduction of him.

Take, for example, a telling illustration that has deep layers of meaning: my students were given the option of reading *Naked Lunch*. A totally adolescent book full of homosexuality, perversion, and drug use, the novel has been excoriated, banned, and revered by generations of rebellious youth. So you would think my students would be interested. Not true. I even showed the film in class, which was much more coherent than the book. I wanted to see if I could spark their interest. Three kids fell asleep during the movie.

Afterward, when I asked the class about the use of metaphor, their clean young faces remained blank. The students always looked like that. Like there was nothing going on inside their heads. Maybe they all wore expressionless masks simply to avoid being called on. I struggled to keep them involved, but I found myself lecturing on assignments instead of discussing their views with them. They were missing out on so much.

"Metaphors, people? Mojito," I said, startling him out of a

dazed reverie. He had his hands behind his head, staring up at the pockmarked ceiling. This annoyed me. "Please share with the class the most memorable aspects of the story itself, and describe for us how this is a metaphor for the novelist's own life circumstances."

I was speaking of William Burroughs' closeted homosexuality and lifelong drug addiction, of course, and how he imposed his own bohemian subversion on the story.

Mojito shifted his lazy eyes to mine. "The most important scene in the film is when he shoots his wife in the head. In real life, Burroughs killed his wife in a Mexican bar. They were wasted when he told her to perform their William Tell act. She balanced a glass on her head and he aimed a handgun at it, fired. *Boom.* He shot too low. Hit her in the head."

The kids who hadn't bothered to read the book flipped through it. Others took out their phones and googled. They murmured to one another until I shushed them.

"So what's the metaphor?" I asked Mojito.

When he tossed his head, his hair fell gracefully around his neck. It gently touched his shoulders, and shone like spun gold under the fluorescent lights of the classroom. "Culpable homicide. The character was killing bugs, his wife, himself. Through the whole story, book and film, the protagonist twists the narrative of who he is, what he's about. Why do lots of readers get confused? Because he's unreliable, he's lying. He's even lying to himself."

I nodded. "Good." I smiled at him but he did not return the smile. I turned to the class. "Burroughs wrote the novel, his first successful book actually, after his wife's death. He claimed he had *no choice but to write his way out*. Does anybody know what he meant by that?"

"He wanted to heal himself from the pain of losing her?" one of the girls offered.

"Yes, and...?" I waited for more. Scanned the classroom, waiting. But nobody spoke up.

Then Mojito said, "And he had to keep the lie going. Why he killed his spouse. And how it happened. And how he was not to blame."

That stopped me for a moment. I hadn't thought of it that way. Very interesting conclusion. I nodded, smiled at him again. This time our eyes met, locked.

I felt the zing in my loins. My lord.

I turned away and said, "Let's move on. How was the novel influenced by the author's friendship with Kerouac? Who's read *On the Road*?"

When I looked out at the class, only Mojito had his hand raised.

So you see, there it was. He was young. He was beautiful. He could engage with me. And somehow, he knew he had me. He intuited what kind of madwoman I was. And that day in class, when he saw that I knew *he* knew, he shrugged those graceful shoulders and grinned.

I emitted a tiny gasp of perverse delight.

So there I was, at his house, a guest of his father. "Come on in, Dr. O," Mojito said, flashing that wily smile.

He'd stressed the *O*. His gray-blue eyes, so like his father's, sparkled with intense interest. And I could see in them and in his cocky grin a knowing sexuality. He stepped back to make room for me to enter the manse.

As I passed by him, I accidentally brushed against his taut body. Sweat, a gym smell mixed with a fresh baked bread aroma. When I inhaled his boyish scent, that torrid odor, slim tears came to my eyes. I felt the deep dark writhing of desire. And I felt alive in a live world.

The house was typical maximum space filled with minimalist luxury. There were the prerequisite thirty-foot ceilings and wall-length windows, oversize crystal chandeliers and sparse high-end furniture. Abstract oils hung on the stark white walls, most by the kind of post-postmodern artists who have huge followings in Paris and New York. A small, dark, uniformed maid dragging a vacuum cleaner glanced up as we passed by.

"We can sit outside," Mojito said while I gawked at the interior landscape.

I nodded, so he led me through sliding glass doors out to a lush garden. The brick patio was spotless, as if it had been recently swept. Mojito indicated a round glass table and several high-backed chairs. I could barely focus, my mind flitting everywhere at once. Above and over everything, Mojito. Mo-hee-toe.

His father was not yet at the table. My heartbeat pulsed in my ears like waves crashing on the shore. Was this a plan of some kind? To get me alone? And then what?

I sat, crossed my legs slowly, looked around. Trees, blooming flowers, a vast green expanse of golf-course lawn. No yacht, no helicopter, but an Olympic-size infinity pool overlooked the Waterway. In the distance, an osprey called out, swooping for fish. The Intracoastal was white-waved, choppy. Gleaming boats motored past.

The bouquet in the middle of the glass table was two feet tall and swimming with scents. Delicate yellow African lilies, bright orange birds of paradise, brimming branches of pink oleander. Ghost orchids. Red and white long-stemmed roses.

"You like the garden?" Mojito asked.

I looked at him. The way the sun lit up his fine features. Such an Adonis.

"Beautiful," I said. "Very beautiful."

My voice shook slightly. This made him smile.

"About that paper on *The Waste Land*," my student began, his low voice a purr in my ear.

I braced myself for a litany of complaints. *The poems are indecipherable. I don't understand the language. Was Eliot insane?*

But Mojito's voice was rich with something fresh. Exuberance, perhaps. Passion? "I love the book. I plan to finish the paper today. This afternoon. I can't wait 'til you read it."

His excitement did not seem false. I stared at him. He returned my gaze. Mojito, oh Mojito.

So that was that, you see. Because when I looked into his eyes, the gray-blue sea took me. And the waves were stronger than I, wilder, roaring then hissing as they came for me, dragging me under and sloshing over my face. I was instantly, fatally, swept away.

The patio door to the pool area slid open and Mr. Mojito stepped out. He was dressed in white slacks creased down the middle and a periwinkle blue polo shirt. He beamed that genuine smile of his, sending it all the way across the yard, communicating clearly his pleasure in seeing me.

"I will leave you to my father," the son said, his face clouding over.

The sun receded, casting shadows. I felt my flesh goosebump when he stood and walked away. He grew smaller and smaller until he disappeared inside the house.

4

Mr. Mojito entertained me all afternoon. As I drove down the narrow drive to the gate, I had to admit, he'd been wonderful. Engaging. Funny. Well-mannered. I'd enjoyed myself in his company. The seafood salad he served us was light, fresh, delicious. The wine was excellent and profuse. All in all, the old man was a perfect gentleman. Good looking and educated, charming. He acted attentive, interested in me. He laughed at my jokes.

Apparently, he was intent on wooing me.

As the gate slid open before me, I snickered, a little tipsy. Too bad he wanted me, eh? Too, too bad.

Oh, I connected with Mr. Mojito intellectually, and I learned that we were simpatico on many levels. We found agreement when discussing our frustrations with the contemporary political situation, our fears about the spread of terrorism, and the rampant gun violence afflicting our young. Yet my loins slept peacefully while we talked. Nothing stirred down there. Even when he brought the conversation around to books. This was over a delightful mango-avocado sorbet and a wonderful French Chablis. Nothing like the California whites I was used to, the vintage he served was crisp and clean. And, I am sure, ultra-expensive.

When he told me he was reading *The Wide Sargasso Sea*, I choked on a spoonful of the iced dessert. What? Why?

"Oh, I've always enjoyed the author. And this book is so rich. I love the poetry of the wanton tropics, the lusty and doomed love," he explained.

I was speechless. A man who read Jean Rhys? For fun?

"Her use of language is unusual," I said, setting my spoon down on the table. "If she tried to publish that novel now, no one would touch it." I ought to know. No publisher would touch mine.

"That's such a shame," he said, staring at me intently. "Perhaps that explains my attachment to older literature. And my detachment from fiction produced after, say, the 1990s." He hesitated, as if rethinking his words. "Although I could use your guidance in the matter. Perhaps you can steer me to some inspiring contemporary novelists?"

"Maybe. I can always try."

We smiled at one another. Shyly, like kids on a first date who discover they might want to have a second. How sweet.

He shared a bit about himself. Born in Morocco, educated in Lima, then college in France. He had wanted to be a university professor, a poet, a writer. But he was too much of a pragmatist. His money came from family with defined ideas for their only son's future. Law. The family firm. He hated the work and, after his parents' deaths, he'd sold his partnership and taken early retirement. Now he ran a small hedge fund. "For friends," he explained.

Yeah. Friends with millions.

He was sixty. I didn't ask, I googled him on my phone when he went inside to fetch our second bottle of wine.

Sixty. The number sent nasty chills down my spine. I

couldn't imagine being with a man that old. Being attracted to someone headed for nothing but physical decline. As I was.

The luncheon, however, was pleasant. He was a charmer, and I was happy to be charmed.

When I was leaving, passing through the white-on-white foyer, Mojito called down to me. He stood at the top of the polished wood staircase that led to the second floor. "See you at school," he said casually before his father whisked me out the front door.

Like a true gentleman, Mr. Mojito walked me out.

I would look forward to seeing the boy in class, was what I was thinking as we tromped down the steps. Really, that was all I wanted to think about. But when we got to my car, Mr. Mojito took my hand in his soft palms. He held it gently for a moment, then pressed my fingers to his lips. His eyes searched mine. Did I want him the way he wanted me?

No, I did not.

I smiled, thanked him for the lovely afternoon. And what did I feel? I felt nothing.

"I will call you, Ms. O'Hale," he said in that calm cultured voice of his. Then he opened the car door for me, held it as I took my seat. "You're such delightful company."

Right. Luckily, he did not have access to all the delights inside my head.

He shut the door and stood back, watching me as I rolled away. I peered in the rearview when I reached the front gate. He was still standing in the driveway, watching.

I drove slowly down A1A. The fat sun hung low in the sky, casting lingering light over the teal and navy-blue ocean. Sailboats sped along. Gulls and pelicans drafted, coasting silently. Yes, one thing was clear: I had no interest in the father.

But as I approached my condo building, pink in the late sun, an intriguing thought slipped through a crack in the wall I had erected in my mind: *one Mojito, two Mojito*. If I dated the dad, then I could see the son on a regular basis. I would be around him on weekends, in the evenings for dinner. We would all go on vacation together. I could accompany them when Mojito went to tour Yale, Harvard, Columbia. I would become a friend. An intimate friend.

My heart, which had returned to its natural rhythm during the sedate afternoon with Mr. Mojito, kicked at my ribcage. It wanted out. It wanted to run free, party hardy, then wallow in the ruins.

I pulled into my parking space under the car tent. The engine ticked as I sat there in the dusky warmth. I closed my eyes to the forest green hue seeping through the canvas shade and imagined a life with the Mojitos. Days spent swimming in their pristine pool, lying on the umbrellaed chaises reading aloud. Plath, Eliot, Whitman. Nights spent laughing over candlelit dinners, our eyes meeting across the mahogany dining table. First class seats on flights to London, Venice, Tokyo. The three of us. It could be done. I could see it.

Enveloped in a romantic daze, I wandered up the four flights of stairs to my apartment. I would have to go through the father to get to the son. But what would be so difficult about that? The old man already wanted me. I could make all his dreams come true, then focus on my own.

Zora greeted me at the door. "Fat fool," I said to her as she wrapped her soft body around my ankles. "You been up to your tricks while I've been gone?"

She meowed, flashed her green grape eyes.

Okay, so I did have a cat. Like all the spinsters do. Still, I didn't sit around petting my cat while I drank herb tea. Cats are too independent for that nonsense, and I preferred drinks with more kick.

"You want food?" I said to my pretty black cat, who switched her tail madly and, I swear, cocked her head. "You looking for a handout? Again?"

After hunting down my other cat, a shy little thing named Pearl, I gave them a good snuggle. Then I fed them. While they chowed down, I grabbed a half-empty carton of California Cab out of the fridge and retreated to the balcony with my laptop. But I was unable to write and, compared to the vintage I'd been enjoying earlier, the wine tasted bad. Like cardboard and smoked plastic.

I removed my reading glasses and closed my eyes, daydreaming about spending the rest of my life with the Mojitos. Yes, I decided, this might be a most brilliant idea. The father was accommodating. And Mojito was...well, he was amazing.

Here is another illustrative incident from school. As often as I could, I would squeeze into the required curriculum my own ideas on literature and culture. Most of what I taught was clearly defined by the school administration to conform to state requirements. However, I would take any opportunity I could to speak of more important issues than old-fashioned morality and social hierarchies. I wanted to teach kids about the new forms of feminism and racism, discuss underground class warfare and subversive rebellion. I felt it was my duty to point out the philosophical highpoints to be found in classic modern and post-modern literature. I thought this was important. Who else was going to give them the truth about the underclass, about women's power? Nobody.

Yet, whenever I broke free of the curriculum and digressed into cultural critique, the students remained passive. When I asked if they had questions or comments, they were silent. Blank faces all around. Still, I persisted.

"Now don't get the wrong idea, I'm not assigning this novel," I told the class one afternoon when post-lunch sleepiness reigned and eyes were at half mast around the hot little classroom. "So don't run home to tell Mommy and Daddy that I did." I held up *Baise-Moi* by French extremist feminist Virginie Despentes. "But this novel will wake you right up, and shake some of you up as well."

Two girls in the front row leaned in. The dark cover photo of a teenage punk with wild piercings had grabbed their interest. "What does *Baise-Moi* mean?" one of them asked.

"The English translation is something like...*fuck me*," I said.

The class laughed. I had their attention.

"If this were *my* school and I could expose you to the subject matter *I* think most important, you'd be reading this novel. And we'd screen the underground film based on the book. But real life?" I shrugged. "It's just not like that. So you'll have to do what you will in your own time."

I often said things like this. Tossing out seeds, saying they could plant them in their own imagination gardens. If they *had* imagination gardens.

I started to put the book back in my shoulder bag.

"What's it about?" the girl in the front row asked.

I hesitated, still holding the novel in my hand. How could I word this so it didn't sound like a feminist manifesto? The kids looked down on feminism, considered it outdated and undesirable, a synonym for pointless man-hating.

"It's about rape revenge," a boy said. I looked up. Mojito. "About two French prostitutes who pair up to kill guys and basically go on a wild violence spree. After being raped and otherwise oppressed."

How did he know this? I tilted my head at him. "Did you read the book or see the film?" I asked.

His blue-gray eyes regarded me calmly. "Both. The film is deeply disturbing. The book is very well written. Especially considering the author was uneducated and working as a hooker when she wrote it."

I nodded, impressed beyond words. My lord.

One of the boys in the back spoke in a faux whisper. "Kiss teacher's ass much, bro?"

Mojito had the maturity to ignore the remark, but his face pinkened.

I composed my thoughts quickly and said, "The book and movie were condemned as pornography in France, the U.S., and elsewhere. The subject matter is dark and dirty, all right. So it's not easy reading, and the film is hard to watch. Very violent, a lot of graphic sex. But the takeaway is this, class: if women were less docile, less victimized and more violent in their behavior, the impact on the culture could be significant. I am not in any way advocating violence as a solution to a problem, people. Okay? But if women could kill their rapists, I wonder what would happen to the rape statistics."

The two girls in front sat back suddenly in their chairs. I heard whispering, spoke above it.

"Just think about it. What does TV teach you about gender roles in this post-postmodern society of ours? That real men go out and commit violence. Right? But women? Women go shopping. Or out to lunch with girlfriends."

Someone said, "Yeah, like in *Girls* or *Sex and the City*."

"What about Angelina Jolie?" another girl said. She was referring to the actress's role in the film *Salt*, I imagined.

Veering off track, one of the boys recounted the plot of the first season of *True Detective*. I loved that show. Terrific nihilism in that dialogue. But what if it had featured two women detectives? What if women behaved more like men—in entertainment and in real life? What then?

The discussion continued for a bit. I smiled to myself as I tucked the book in my bag. Then I quieted the class and said, "Okay, everybody. We need to resume the discussion we were having on *A Farewell to Arms*. Open to the last page, please, and read the final lines."

Their eyes returned to the asleep at the wheel position. I told them how Hemingway had rewritten the ending more than thirty times. To get the words just right. I thought this was an interesting fact. But I was, once again, speaking only to myself. Their heads were bowed, and nobody responded.

Then I caught his eye. Mojito nodded. *I approve*, was what he seemed to be saying. *You're interesting.*

Right back atcha, was what I was thinking in that moment.

At home with my cats after a pleasant afternoon spent with his attentive father, I dwelled on thoughts about this intelligent, gorgeous, young, oh so young, man. It expanded to fill my mind. My body. Eventually it would expand enough to fill my whole world.

Mojito. Mo-hee-toe.

5

"**D**o you have family in South Florida?" Mr. Mojito asked me as we drove several towns south to a waterfront restaurant he had chosen for our first dinner date. "Parents? Children?"

I shook my head. Children? That was a laugh. Whenever other people's diaper-heavy toddlers wandered near, I wanted to yell out to the beleaguered parents, *Call them off*.

At least until they were eleven. Or, better yet, seventeen.

Dusk had darkened up and the cool wind rippled through my hair. The Rolls slid through the evening like silk across bare skin. The night sky vibrated with stars, and crickets clicked in the rustling palm trees. What could be better than this?

Mojito the son at the wheel, of course.

I feigned solemnity. "Like your son, I was an only child," I lied. I was no longer in touch with brother Hugh. He hadn't approved of my lifestyle for decades. Then for a change of pace I told a truth. "My parents are dead. They died in a tragic auto accident."

Tragic for them, but not for me. I had inherited a nice pile of money. Which explained my condo on the beach, the easygoing lifestyle I enjoyed on a paltry high school teacher's salary. It had been years since probate concluded in my favor and I was, of course, fully recovered from the loss. They'd probably been at one another's throats when they rolled their SUV out in the Everglades. I did not miss them.

Still, I made a sorry face for my date. He reached over to pat my hand.

I kept up the farce. "Losing your parents helps you empathize with young people. How difficult it is for them to grow up and cut their ties." My voice was low, appropriately toneless. The truth was, my parents were not loving people. Both were cold and withholding. Mean to one another, indifferent with the rest of the world. Including me. Only in death had they given me what I really needed. Money. And the kind of freedom that comes with having some.

But that lovely little windfall had diminished to a sad wisp. The most recent recession had taken a greedy bite out of what was left of my holdings, and the resale value of my condo had plummeted. I'd begun to think about finding a new source of disposable income.

And there I was, with a man who wanted me, on the way to his chichi country club.

"That's such a shame," he said. There was real feeling in his voice. "My son still struggles with the loss of his mother more than a decade ago. She had addiction issues and, after she left us, her life went downhill. He lost her early on, but she died more recently. Just a few years ago." He shook his head. "If he were to lose me as well, I am sure that would be incredibly difficult for him."

Yes. And no. Still, I looked sympathetic and nodded my head.

"After my wife disappeared, I was depressed. Her problems were my problems, and I thought I could help her. But she fled.

And the rest is the classic drug addict's story of self-destruction. Thinking about it makes me sad. But I focus on my son's needs and this keeps me going." He sighed, then added, "It must be more difficult for you to soldier on when times are challenging. Being all alone in this difficult world."

I nodded again. I felt like one of those bobbleheads stupid people have on their dashboards. I was thinking how, if Mr. Mojito died, it would be hard for his son. But also quite rewarding financially. As the sole heir to a tidy fortune, Mojito would never have to work a day in his life.

But that would not be good for young Mojito. The boy had ambitions. He was the kind of person who wanted to work hard, to achieve. He strived to learn and excel. The motivated student, a teacher's rare gem. Most kids would rather get high. They couldn't care less.

Mojito cared. Like father, like son. Or so I thought at the time.

"Your son's paper on *The Waste Land* was remarkable," I said as we pulled up to the Pepto-Bismol pink guard gate for the Boca Raton Private Club. "I've never read a student paper that thoughtful before. Especially on one of Eliot's most challenging works."

I was downplaying it. Truth was, his paper had been stunning. Significantly better than the papers my college students had written. Too bad Mojito turned it in late. This necessitated deducting points from what would have been a perfect score.

"I know. I read it. I liked how his language emulated that of the poet," Mr. Mojito said. We were waiting for the Mercedes coupe in front of us to be ushered inside the gated compound. "I thought that was remarkable in itself."

"Agreed. I admired his use of dreamlike metaphor, the dark humor. Really an A-plus paper." Talking about Mojito with his father was strangely electrifying. Like chatting about a crush with a girlfriend who shared your emotional investment. "He's got the ability to rip away the ordinary. I like that."

Mr. Mojito turned to face me. His eyes shone with something. Admiration? Trust? Desire? "He is brilliant, my son. I can see that you see it too. But I must tell you, I'm not sure how to guide him now, at this delicate age. On the verge of adulthood. Maybe you can provide me with your learned insight on this?"

Learned insight? I wanted to teach the boy what he could do to make me scream, and the father was asking me for babysitting tips?

I almost giggled.

Fortunately, the car behind us honked rudely and the moment passed. Boca people are the worst. Had I been alone, I would have lifted my arm in the international fuck off salute.

I restrained myself as we rolled forward to the garish pink guard box. A burly security moron asked for a name and intentions. The resort restricts membership in a multitude of ways, keeping the grounds reserved for use by the ultra-rich. Believe me, they don't just usher in any old Rolls that happens to drive up.

Mr. Mojito provided his club membership ID. The guard stepped back inside his air-conditioned booth, then returned wearing a subservient grin. "Go right in, Mr. Mojito. Sorry to keep you waiting."

My date smiled in that pleasant man-to-man way which did not share in another's stupidity but did not condemn it either. The guard tipped his cap respectfully and backed away.

Approved and appropriately kowtowed to, we passed through the black iron gate and drove slowly up a long silky drive to the gleaming white portico. The club was divided into two sections: the old historic original building, which oozed class, and a spidering sprawl of modern, ornate, and truly ugly add-ons.

A microcosm of the city itself. Of the American culture.

When I expressed this thought out loud, my date laughed. "You are so observant, and amusingly mordant," he said, warming me with an approving smile.

That smile of his. It seemed so genuine, yet deeply masculine. Shy and confident at the same time. He could change it at will. It was like a weapon, a tease, a seductive lure. How many women had he bedded with that smile?

I pictured him forty years younger: Mojito, but with darker hair and skin. That lantern jaw, the steely eyes. Wow. The father at seventeen might have been even more sexy than his son.

Too bad he was an old man. At sixty, he was nothing to me but an obstacle. A roadblock on the way to my quarry. Unless I took charge of the situation, in which case he would become the means to a very satisfying end.

A teenage valet in pressed white shorts opened my door and held out a slim hand. I clasped it, looking up into lively bleached blue eyes. A cutie-pie. I grinned and allowed him to slide me from the leather interior of the car.

Directly behind the boy, Mr. Mojito stood waiting for me. The look on his face? Anticipatory devotion mixed with animal lust. The old man was smitten.

Poor Mr. Mojito. I knew myself. And I would not be merciful.

The restaurant was cavernous, brightly lit, and full of chattering elderly women. Perfumed dowagers in floppy hats flashing their chunky gold, their bulky diamonds. Old women disturb me even more than old men do. When I shivered with disgust, my observant date thought the air conditioning was too cold for me. He suggested we dine out on the terrace.

Anything to get away from the nursing-home crowd.

A young black-frocked hostess seated us at a table under a yawning fig tree. We sat next to one another, alone out there except for the attentive wait staff. The moon was a smiling crescent overhead, a sea wind coming in off the Atlantic. All around us, hidden from view, the crickets sang for a mate. And for their own death, I assume. Insects die so soon after mating.

Thinking about this, I had to hide my smile. But Mr. Mojito caught it, and reached for my hand. "Happy?" he asked, boyish in the soft light.

"Yes. I like to be outside," I said lamely. God, I needed a drink. "And it's such a nice evening."

He nodded. "I'm glad I could bring you here. I'm so grateful you had the time to see me tonight."

The time? I had plenty of that. It was the desire I lacked.

Still, with enough drink in me, I was sure I could stick to my plan. One Mojito, two Mojito, I reminded myself as he perused the wine list and discussed Italian vintages with the tuxedoed sommelier.

The meal lasted for hours. I listened carefully as my date opened up about his drug-addled wife, the turmoil that followed her desertion. Single parenting, his son's emotional issues after his mother's departure, and again after her death. He told me about his love for the water, fishing, sailing, all ways to escape his problems at home. He lightened up after that, and we discussed favorite authors, movies, music. We laughed about Florida culture (none worth mentioning), and our own literary aspirations (similarly pathetic). He considered himself a failed poet; I told him about my ongoing struggles with publishing my fiction.

We bonded, as they say.

Well, *he* bonded. *I* drank. Aperitif? Why not. I would need to numb up for what was sure to follow the espresso and crème brûlée.

He was not guileless, that's for sure. He had set his high beams on me and his intentions were brightly lit. As Mr. Mojito dined and wined me, he held my hand under the candlelit tablecloth. My hand, as a matter of fact, was in his lap. He was aroused, and he wanted me.

I kept drinking. The attentive waiters refilled our glasses without interrupting our hushed conversation. I ate little, drank more. He did the opposite and, because of this foresight, was able to confidently guide me upstairs to the suite he had reserved for the night.

Rich old men tend to think they can get whatever they want. And in this particular instance, he was right. Mostly.

He held the thick oak door for me and I sashayed inside, hips moving seductively. Perhaps also a bit drunkenly. The living room was garishly luxurious with leopard print wall hangings, a ruby-red brocade couch and loveseat, and a black leather wet bar. The bedroom was even more wild with a bearskin rug and a four-poster canopied bed in tiger stripes.

As soon as he shut the door behind us, I was in his arms.

Within minutes, my dress was unzipped, his hands sliding around on my bare flesh. His mouth was wet, hungry. He smelled of garlic and decay.

This is where my story turns embarrassing. Sex with the father of the object of your heart's desire is, well, humiliating. I wanted Mojito, and here I was, spreading my legs for his aged father. That's just plain weird. I lay there on the pale pink Egyptian cotton sheets, gutted like a naked fish, running my hands through his graying hair while he made all sorts of primitive sounds above me. Soon enough, it was over.

Thank God.

"I love you, Cathriona O'Hale," he told me later, after I had thrown up a little in the black-and-white-tiled bathroom. He gently cleaned the vomit from my lips with a damp facecloth. "I want to marry you."

I hiccupped and more overpriced Brunello sloshed up and into my mouth. I swallowed hard. "Okay," I managed to say without barfing.

His face brightened with a mix of boyish joy and carnal desire. Obviously, we weren't done yet with the sex. I gulped and smiled, trying to look sexy. It wasn't easy.

I will spare you the gory details, but let me say this: Mr. Mojito had an unusually high testosterone level, a bit of a magic wand, and an acrobat's ability to manipulate our bodies into positions that were both excruciating and impressive. I was sore for the entire week following.

But we were, it seemed, informally engaged. He confirmed this the next day by texting me that he loved me, claiming he had already ordered an engagement ring. *One suitable for a woman as intelligent, beautiful, and loving as you*, he texted.

I had to laugh. Right. If he knew whose face I imagined while he made love to me, he might have saved himself whatever he'd spent on that ring. He could've invested the money in his son's future.

Which, in a way, he had. But not in the way he'd wanted or expected to.

Like I said, I had no mercy. None.

6

A t my request, Mr. Mojito kept our engagement a secret. The man was trustworthy. A true gentleman. And indefatigable in bed.

No man is perfect.

For weeks, I continued the sex charade with the father while my loins wept for the son. Such a harlot. I was both disgusted with myself and wildly elated. I had snagged the old man without even trying. And soon enough, I would be living chez Mojito. Close to my love. Lying in bed in the room just down the hall from his teenage bedroom, with its wall posters and piles of dirty underwear. Sigh.

One rainy afternoon when I was on my way home from school, Mr. Mojito called. I knew it had to be something important. Usually he texted me from wherever he was, short messages only. He was a businessman, moving money by the trash bag. I knew enough not to try to communicate with him while he was with his clients. Besides, the less we talked during the week, the better I felt about what I was doing. He was a nice person who genuinely cared for me. There was only so much of that I could take. Usually, he texted me where to meet him and what time, then I would make sure to be there. Occasionally, he picked me up at my place. Once or twice, he came in for a nightcap and stayed the night. He wanted a key, so I gave one to him. Whatever he suggested, I agreed to. I made myself available for him, serviced him as he wished. In a way, I enjoyed the docility. Such a delightful ruse.

Besides, every woman loves a fascist. To quote Plath. Who stuck her head in the oven when her beloved bad boy went astray. No man is perfect, she should have known that.

"This is a surprise," I said when I picked up.

"Cathriona, I need you to come to the house tonight. At seven."

He sounded breathless, which wasn't like him. The man was always cucumber chill. I had never heard him less than Zen calm, except in the throes of passion.

"Are you all right? Is everything okay?" My concerns immediately turned to Mojito. "Is this about Mojito?"

"He knows, Cath. He found out."

My heart bobbed up my throat, choking me. I had realized, of course, the moment was inevitable. From the beginning, telling Mojito had been part of the long-term plan. But what a hurdle I faced. Making him understand I wanted him but was marrying his dad. Would he desire me after knowing I had laid naked in his old man's arms? I was counting on deep-seated father/son competition to come to my aid. But would primitive Oedipal yearnings prevail?

"How?" I asked, pulling off the road into the empty parking lot of a sleazy strip mall. Pawn shop, consignment store, one-minute massage. How did these people manage to pay the rent anyway? "Did you tell him?"

"Of course not," my fiancé reassured me. "You and I agreed to present the news at the appropriate time."

We were going to wait until the end of the school year. To avoid any discomfort in class. My idea, and Mr. Mojito had bought it.

He sighed deeply. "Now I'm at a loss."

His voice was soft, like he was emotionally shaken. Was he afraid I would blame him, be angry with him? How sweet.

I cleared my throat, said tightly with a bit of a growl, "So how...?"

"We were seen by a classmate, it appears. And we were *behaving romantically*. Or so Mojito has just texted me. You must come over tonight. I need you to be there when I tell him about our plans."

His voice had a tone of desperation. This made me giddy with joy.

"I'm busy tonight," I said, pretending to be cross. "I really hate to cancel a parent conference on such short notice. But..." I paused, allowing him to squirm. Really, I had nothing on the agenda. But this was such fun. I sighed loudly. "Okay."

He oozed gratitude, I feigned irritation, then we hung up.

I had the father where I wanted him. But the son would be a much bigger challenge.

Before pulling out of the strip mall, I made a quick call to my girl at the hair salon. I would need to look my best. Sexy, youthful, and as unmotherly as humanly possible.

The traffic was thick, the afternoon heat thicker. Too humid for what passed for autumn in South Florida. I drummed my fingers on the steering wheel, turned down the AC. I was really uptight. The tension with Mojito had cranked to an unbearable level. His clear eyes watched my every move when I lectured in class, and a tiny smile played on his lips whenever I called on him. He almost seemed to be mocking my lust. Yet matching it with his own. I was wet from the excitement, the alluring taboo, and he seemed to pick up on this. If he brushed against me now,

I wasn't sure I could control myself. Going to his home tonight and spending time with father and son would be excruciating. Dangerous. Electrifying.

The traffic eased and I sped up. I told myself to be strong. My most intoxicating release had to wait until we were alone together after I was his father's wife. Oh God, oh God. My depravity had grown monstrous, the anticipation unlike anything I had ever experienced.

My imagination played out wildly whenever I had sex with Mr. Mojito. While I pretended he was his son, he devoured me with insatiable delight. One morning at sunrise, he told me I was the most ardent lover he had ever known. "Your passion is contagious," he whispered when he was finally spent. I lay beside him, my eyes closed, my mind elsewhere. "I am so in love with you," he added.

He was indeed. Too bad, too bad. For such a brilliant and successful man, his ability to read people was certainly subpar.

As I turned into the small asphalt lot for the hair salon, I realized what I would be facing in just a few hours. I would see Mojito again in a private setting. Not at school, but on his home turf. Where he had so much control. He could do anything to me there. Anything.

A terrible laugh escaped from between my dry lips. I so needed a drink.

Luckily, the hair salon was called Tipsy Tina's for a very good reason. Tina served wine and champagne. While getting my hair done, I would certainly allow myself to imbibe a few glasses of the bubbly. After all, I had to fortify. I needed to play this out perfectly. I would have to remain in character all evening in front of Mojito. Attractively aloof. Desirable but untouchable and, tragically, spoken for.

I locked the car and headed for the salon. My heart fluttered around my chest like a bird in a bone cage. The anticipation was ruining my nervous system. If my passion was so captivating while I was only pretending to be with Mojito, what would I be like when I was finally in bed with my love? And when would I be able to act on my one true desire?

A tear rolled down my cheek. A tear of horrible lust.

7

Properly fortified, styled, perfumed, and draped in my slinkiest dress, I drove to the Mojitos' at seven. No need to identify myself via intercom as the shiny gate to heaven had already been opened for me. Such a lure, and a perfect metaphor for my life right then.

I parked between the Rolls and a blood-red BMW, then checked my face in the rearview mirror. Did I have time for a nip from my flask? My made-up face frowned at me. I ignored my disapproving self and reached for the thermos of emergency tequila.

Behind me, footsteps crunched on the tiny stones of the driveway. I swallowed fast and tucked the offending container in the cup holder, pretending to search my purse. Outside the car window, a shadow loomed, blocking what was left of the day's sun.

Mojito.

The tequila burned in my mouth.

He stared in at me, his handsome face unreadable. His lean arms were crossed. He was wearing a white oxford shirt and slim-fit cargo shorts. Nice.

I mouthed, *What?*

He shook his head and stepped back so that I could open the car door and slide out. Was he going to accost me in the driveway, without his father's protective presence? My knees trembled. The tequila boiled all the way down to my gut.

I searched my bag for a breath mint, ducking his eyes. "Hey. You decide on an author for your term paper yet?"

The little metal box of mints eluded me. I fished around in my cluttered purse, grateful for the distraction. He remained silent, a seething mass of youthful manhood. I felt ill with guilt and desire.

His silence caused all the tight filaments of my muscles to tense even more. I was vibrating like a violin string. Finally, I gave up and looked at him. He was still staring at me. His eyes were stormy. An angry sea tossed itself around in there. A gale force wind blew my way. I almost toppled over. My insides felt singed.

"You have something you want to tell me?" His voice was the hiss of waves frothing on raked sand.

I shrugged, popping two Altoids and easing by him to head for the front steps. "About what?" Inside my head, a riptide pulled me apart strand by pulsating strand.

Suddenly, a hand grabbed my shoulder. His touch killed me, it really did. Through the silk of my thin dress, his palm burned against my hot skin. He was passionate like me, not cool like his father. My heart knocked against my chest, begging for release.

I pulled away. "Don't touch."

He'd broken the student/teacher barrier with that move. He had seduced me with his youth, his lusting eyes, he'd branded me with the heat of his touch. I could not lie to myself, he would try to take me soon and soon he would have me. Because he would devour me whole. Whole, with all the unstoppable force of a young man's desire. Which was what I wanted. It was all I wanted, had ever wanted.

But not there. And not then.

"You can't do this," he said in a choked voice. "You can't see my father." The way he said *father*, it was like he was spitting out broken rocks.

And I'd thought the two of them had such a good relationship.

I shrugged and headed for the front door. "Come inside. We'll talk with your dad about this." I kept going until I heard Mojito's footsteps on the gravel behind me, then I stopped. "It will all work out fine," I reassured him over my shoulder.

He did not respond. But he caught up to me, then pressed against me, his lean torso like a flame licking my back. His aroma was feral. I breathed deep, smiling to myself. Heady stuff.

I moved on and up the steps. At the landing, he reached around me for the heavy door, held it open for me. "After you," he said, his tone dripping with sarcasm. "Or should I say, after *Dad*?"

I had to laugh. Like his father, I had Mojito where I wanted him. One Mojito, two Mojito. As easy as drinking a double shot of Mezcal.

As we entered the grand foyer, I paused to allow my student to lead the way. Even as my stomach lurched about like a drunk on a bender, I ached for another drink. Thank God Mr. Mojito was a wine connoisseur. If I'd had to face this little party sober, I wouldn't have made it past the front hallway.

Mojito led me across the pristine living area to the sliding glass doors that led out to the pool deck. Our footsteps echoed in the high-ceilinged room. The house was quiet. No maids with vacuums, no piped-in music, no bustling kitchen noises. There were no wafting dinner scents either. Their mansion sat there like a supermodel, looking perfect, signifying nothing *but* perfect. That is, perfect emptiness. The air conditioning was so low, so cold, it made me shiver.

Out back, we walked around the tranquil swimming pool, the still water that strange blue color of Popsicles. The lawn spread before us, golfish and smooth, ending abruptly at the glittering Waterway. A motor yacht sped by, followed by a chunky fishing boat. Lights were already on across the Intracoastal in the pink and white mansions that lined the banks like petits fours.

I followed Mojito down a slate walkway to the dock. No boat awaited us, just three wooden deck chairs facing the water. His father sat in one, his back to us. The sun was setting before us with a reassuring orange splash.

I kept my sunglasses on and tried to feign calm. I could hear my heart hitting the wall, bruising itself. In the flash of tangerine light, Mojito glowed with something intangible. I wanted him to stop walking, turn to me, and take me in his arms.

But that would ruin everything. And he was young but not stupid.

He walked past his father to stand twenty feet away at the end of the dock. He kept his back to us and for that I was grateful.

And for those gorgeous buns of his. The view was breathtaking.

With a deep sigh, I dropped into the Adirondack chair next to Mr. Mojito. He kissed me lightly and put a tentative hand on my knee. "We okay?" he asked in a whisper.

I shrugged.

A bottle of red next to his chair was half empty. He leaned forward to pour me a glass. Did I need more fortification? You bet.

We drank our wine in nervous silence while Mojito stewed at the far end of the dock.

"Have you talked about it yet?" I asked my lover.

He nodded. "A little. He's upset."

Mojito turned around and called out to us. "I can hear every word you say. The water amplifies the sound." The sun made him look like a pillar of fire. Burn, baby, burn. "So go ahead and say whatever. I don't give a shit."

Of course he gave a shit. The boy was lit up, aflame with the pain of unspoken desire. I tried not to laugh but I emitted a smothered sound.

Mr. Mojito misunderstood and immediately reached for me. He hugged me close. He smelled of spices, like an older man does just before he goes bad—from age, and inner rot. "Don't worry, darling. I'm not going to end things with us," he said quietly. "He'll come around." Then he raised his voice, even though there was obviously no need. "Have a glass of wine with us, son. Let's discuss this like three sensible adults."

Even though he'd included me in that statement, I felt like a giggly teen. I smirked into my wine, guzzling it to hide my mirth. I tend to laugh when I'm being bad, when I'm heading for trouble. A childish habit.

As Mojito approached, I watched his lean hips sway. Yummy. When he reached us, his groin was right there, at eye level. If I'd leaned forward, I could've grabbed him with my teeth.

He sat down on the other side of his father, who handed him a full glass of wine. Then Mr. Mojito replenished my empty goblet, killing that soldier. He'd go inside soon to fetch another bottle. At that point, I would be alone with his tantalizingly bitter son.

I would wait for that moment with mounting excitement.

In the meantime, Mr. Mojito carefully explained the situation as he saw it. Which was not the way I saw it. Even though he assumed it was. Men are like that, assuming their feelings match your own.

Ha. Little do they know.

"Son, the truth is I fell in love with Cathriona at first sight. At our teacher's conference two months ago. She tried to avoid me, it wasn't professional for her to date me and we both knew that. But finally she relented and we spent that wonderful afternoon together here. You remember. And that's when I knew she felt the same way about me. At our age, son, you know this kind of thing immediately. Perhaps because there's no time to waste with game playing and dithering around."

Oh, if the poor man only knew. All I wanted to do was dither around—with his beloved son.

Mr. Mojito sipped his wine, continued with his warped version of our romance. "We've spent a good deal of quality time together since then. And we're in love. Which means we are not being sexual without taking responsibility. We're lovers because we're *in* love. And we plan to marry. I've bought the ring, but Cath refuses to wear it until school is out. Which is so like her. Always thinking about others' best interests instead of her own."

Yeah, that was me, all right.

Mojito sat there, stiff and silent. The crickets were out in full force. Across the water, someone turned on a stereo. The Stones, *Satisfaction*. A cigarette boat roared by, drowning out the rock music.

Suddenly, Mojito laughed. An old person's life-weary laugh. "Okay, *Dad*," he said, once again ejecting the word with venom. "Make yourself happy. You always do." He swigged his glass of wine, held out the empty goblet. "In the meantime, if you don't mind, can you fill 'er up?"

Mr. Mojito rose from the chair that separated me from Mojito. "I'll get another bottle. Maybe you can talk some sense into the boy, Cath." He said this with a despairing glance my way. Then he left us alone on the dock.

Mistake, mistake.

8

As soon as his father entered the house and we heard the glass door slide shut behind him, Mojito stood. I remained seated, my muscles so taut my feet were cramping. He walked over to stand in front of me. I looked up. It was dark so his face was hard to read, but the lust shone bright in his pretty eyes.

I smiled. *Gotcha.*

He said in a squeaky voice, "Go ahead, *Cath*. Talk sense to *the boy*." Then he leaned down and looked me right in the face. I could smell the alcohol on his breath. "When we both know all you really want to do is fuck me."

My smile faded. He was spoiling the fun. "Shut up. Don't be so crude."

I crossed my legs, kicking him lightly in the shin. He placed his hands on the armrests of my chair. His breath in my face smelled really boozy. Had he been drinking earlier, or was that from the wine? He didn't seem drunk, just pissed off. And desirous beyond understanding. Beyond self-control.

I knew how that felt. Oh yes.

"I know you want me, *Cath*. So what the hell are you doing with dear old Dad?"

I pulled back, but I was trapped in the chair. "Move. You're in my space. Back off or I'll kick you in the balls."

He snorted, then snuck a hand between my knees. "I don't think so."

Uh oh.

His palm warmed my bare thighs. As he worked that hand all the way up the insides of my legs, I didn't flinch. His skin was so hot it felt like my thighs were being ironed. We both held our breath, his eyes locked with mine. Time held still.

When his long fingers reached the dampness at my crotch, he leered. "Is that for me? Or for the old man?"

I shook my head, whispered, "Stop it," but he ignored me. The boy was not like his father. He was not a gentleman. But, just like the old man, he was pushing his way into my life. Aggressive, demanding, taking control.

All traits I could admire. But this was not the plan I had in mind for us.

I did what had to be done and broke the spell. I leaned forward and slapped him across the face. Hard. He reared back.

"When I say stop, I mean now," I scolded.

Shaken, he stared down at me. His face was reddening where I'd whacked him.

I heard the glass doors slide open and without turning around, I knew Mr. Mojito was on his way down the pathway to the dock. I said in a whisper, very slowly, "You have misunderstood my interest in your welfare. I am your teacher. And soon, I will be your stepmother. You and I will have to play by those rules, kiddo."

His auburn eyebrows arched, that familiar smile toying with his full lips. "You think?" he asked lightly. "Because *I* don't think so." He glanced over my head to see how far away his father was, then added under his breath, "I know exactly who you are, Dr. O. I've got you all figured out."

My heart was up in my throat, choking me like a piece of unchewed steak. This was *so* not the way it was supposed to go.

Moments later, Mr. Mojito's reassuring hand was on my shoulder. "You two work things out?"

Mojito flashed a fake grin. "We're on it, Dad."

"I'm glad," his father said. I could hear the relief in his voice.

Mojito didn't look at me, but he sat again while his father poured more wine in our glasses.

I drank way too much after that. I was preoccupied, worried, madly aroused. I had no intention of sleeping with Mr. Mojito though. Not at their house, not that night.

We all behaved well, excessively careful with one another as we talked. We chatted about anything besides our own bizarre and uncomfortable triangle. Mojito put on a good show, I thought. Disinterested yet cooperative. Almost normal.

The sky lightened as the moon came up and Mojito yawned several times. Nobody mentioned dinner and eventually the second bottle was drained. At that point, Mojito excused himself. He had homework to complete. Or so he claimed.

It was, after all, a school night. So I too had an excuse to end the evening.

Mr. Mojito walked me past the pool deck and through the jungled side yard. Overhead, royal palms and bamboo swayed gently in the soft wind. We followed a cedar chip path through the brush to the front of the house, easing out of the thick green tangle that surrounded the mansion. I wasn't fond of the stark interior, but the thick overgrowth that comprised the yard was magnificent.

"I love the wildness of your landscaping," I told my lover. "Was it like this when you bought the place?"

He took my hand and cooled it in his own. "When they built

the house ten years ago, the lot was undeveloped. The builder razed only what he had to in order to erect the house. Kept everything else the way it was. Old Florida trees and underbrush. Sawgrass and cabbage palms. Swampland and mosquitos, although the bugs aren't too bad because of the ocean breezes. This is why I love the place so. I detest the new Florida. All those stripped-out suburban developments with their bland treeless vistas and zero lot lines."

I agreed, then asked him what their previous home had been like. Did you have any life in your house when your wife was living there with you, was what I wanted to ask him.

By this time we had reached my car. He pressed his trim body against mine, kissed me tenderly on the forehead. "That's another story for another night," he said. "Tonight I want to thank you from the bottom of my heart for being here. For coming to my aid. Whatever you said to him, you calmed my son down. It seems he might even be accepting of the situation. You're a marvel, Cathriona."

I kissed his sunken cheek. If he only knew. I was a marvel, all right.

I climbed in my car and started the engine. When he leaned in the window to kiss me on the mouth, to express his love for me, his gratitude, his ardor, I closed my eyes.

You know by now that I am dimly depraved, so you must know whose lips I imagined, whose tongue I pretended was licking at my hungry mouth. The boy was in my blood. He was like an infection, and I was sick with him.

I drove home slowly, careful not to weave. I didn't need a DUI, not now, not ever. In Florida if you lose your driver's license, you lose everything. The cities were designed for cars. Public transportation is a joke. I couldn't afford to get caught when I shouldn't have been behind the wheel.

Fortunately, the local cops were all at Starbucks or Dunkin's.

So I made it home unscathed, made my way upstairs and collapsed on the couch. I would have a humdinger of a headache in the morning. Red wine did that to me.

I wished I had more control. But I didn't. Not with the booze, not with the boys.

Zora started up the usual whining, rubbing her dark fur against my legs. "In a minute, my black beauty," I said. "Let me chill for a moment, please." After she meowed in her most bossy tone, I headed for the kitchen with a sigh.

I was indulging myself in bottled water and preventive Advil when the text came in. I clicked on it without much interest. A goodnight love note from Mr. Mojito, no doubt. But as I chugalugged Zephyrhills and stared at the message on my phone, my pulse sped up. I swallowed hard, choking a little on the water. I stumbled to the kitchen table and sat on one of the wicker chairs.

Mojito?

Yes, my first text ever from my love. He had my number? Yes he did.

I am nothing to you?

What was I supposed to say to that?

I thought carefully. I needed to marry the father first. Then I could express my true feelings for the son. Telling him now would be foolhardy. It would be risky and self-destructive. No matter how good it would feel, it would be bad for both of us.

So I texted back: *Of course not. You are my fiancé's son. And my most brilliant student.*

Then I wept, ladies and gentlemen of the jury. I put my head down on the small glass table in my tidy condo kitchen and I wept.

PART II

THE SPRING

9

On the first Saturday of the nine-day spring break, the boys picked me up at dawn. The day was already hot and humid, even though the sun had just edged up over the horizon. I was sweating a little as I lifted my suitcase into the back of the rental vehicle, a wedding-cake white Cadillac Escalade. When I slid into the passenger seat, I noted the car was fully loaded. We would be traveling in high style. The leather seats were flesh colored and smelled like new moccasins.

I inhaled deeply and grinned at Mr. Mojito. "This is going to be fun."

When I peered over my shoulder at Mojito, he was scrolling on his phone. Mr. Mojito and I rolled our eyes, smiling at one another.

As we pulled out of the condo parking lot and onto A1A, he said over his shoulder, "You can be glued to your phone the whole time, kid. Or you can open your eyes and take a look at the east coast. Your choice. But you might want to be in this dimension instead of the digital one. At least for the next week."

Mojito shrugged. "Whatevs." But he slid the phone into his pocket and turned to look out the window.

. . .

Five hours later, we were still in Florida and Mojito was scrolling. I couldn't blame him. I-95 is insane with traffic until you are well north of West Palm Beach, then it's nothing but citrus groves and discount malls until you get to Jacksonville, where it's traffic hell again until the state line.

This little family road trip had been my idea, but I'd made sure Mr. Mojito believed it was his. After hinting that it would be "fun" to take a long drive up north, that I missed the mountains and adored hiking (I don't like them one bit, actually, as I suffer from a deep-seated phobia of ticks and their lingering viruses), my subtleties had rooted and a plan grew in the old man's brain.

My plan.

"Why don't we go on a road trip?" he'd finally suggested one night over lobster and chilled Chardonnay. We were dining outside on the patio at Oceans 123, a luxury bistro overlooking the crashing waves of the Atlantic Ocean. The moon was full and so was the restaurant. I leaned in to hear what he was proposing, my heart pitter-pattering with a growing excitement. "We can rent an Escalade so we're comfortable and power up the coast. Get out of the tropics for a while. Head for the Blue Ridge mountains. Or Vermont."

I pretended to be surprised and unsure. Sipping my third glass of the light white wine, I cocked an eyebrow and tilted my head. "I'd love to. But what about work?"

He shrugged. "We'll go during spring break. When you have time off. We'll drive as far north as we like, then fly back before school resumes."

He reached for my hand. In the candlelight, his eyes shone. He was so in love with me. I almost felt bad for the man.

I fondled his smooth hand while imitating a woman who would need to weigh the idea of going on a long trip with her fiancé. Then I smiled, shyly, while casting my eyes down. "I think it would be lovely," I said, then looked at him, my face serious. "But we must take Mojito with us. He can't stay home alone for a week. Not at his vulnerable age."

Mr. Mojito's eyes filled and he squeezed my hand. "You are such a loving person, Cathriona. I've never met anyone like you before."

I'm sure he hadn't.

"My son would be fine at home with the help. But yes, let's take him with us. He spends too much time on his phone. He could use a good outing."

I smiled wide as if I had just thought of something. Actually, this had been my next line of offense had Mr. Mojito resisted my request to bring his son on tour with us. Brightening, I sat up straight and said, "I know! We can stop at a few east coast colleges and look over the campus. Maybe take a tour. We can stop at Duke, Princeton. Columbia in New York City. And Harvard maybe?"

Always bait the man with his own ego. In this case, a teacher intimating the brilliance of his only son was like catnip. He snapped it up.

His eyes full of appreciation and desire, Mr. Mojito stood and pulled me halfway to my feet. I leaned across the small table for his kiss, a long sultry romantic smooch.

Behind me, an elderly lady tittered and her grumpy husband muttered under his breath. I was bent so far forward they must have been looking at my panties.

Was I wearing any panties? I couldn't recall.

Oh well. Who cared? The road trip was on.

I looked out the passenger side window at the thick forest alongside the highway. In Georgia the trees were older than most of the palms in Florida, much taller, and a deep rich green. Evergreens. I rolled down the window for a sniff.

"It smells like Christmas," I announced with a smile.

Mr. Mojito rolled down his window and I turned around to look at his son. The phone was still in his pocket and his face had a relaxed look I'd rarely seen before.

Mojito said, "The fresh air feels good. It's cooler here."

"Since it's early March, it probably won't be springtime where we're going. It's still cold up north and even here, in the southern states, it'll be pretty cold at night."

He grinned. "Sounds great."

Oh, Mojito. Those feral teeth, that sexy cleft chin, those lucid blue-gray eyes. I had to turn away, focus my own desirous eyes on the tree-lined road. I was determined to make the boy mine while keeping him at the necessary distance as I continued the romance charade with his dad. It was the only way Mojito and I could be together one day, not as a couple of poor working stiffs, but as lucky lovers living in the kind of material comfort my boy had grown accustomed to.

I was growing accustomed to such luxury myself. And I didn't want to give it up. No, wealth would be the glue that bound us together. Wealth and lust. You shouldn't indulge in one without the other. Not if you wanted something that would last. Which I did. I wanted Mojito to be mine until the cushy sexy *über*-deluxe end.

We stopped in Brunswick to eat lunch at an outdoor barbecue restaurant. We chose a picnic table in the sun where the temperature was a perfect sixty-five degrees. The songbirds in the hundred-foot pines entertained us with their mating calls while the boys ravished their fatty ribs, chowing down like a couple of cavemen. I teased them about being primates. I nibbled on a piece of cornbread and a side of crispy coleslaw, mellowing out with a couple of cans of Pabst.

During the meal, Dad kept a possessive hand on my thigh. Meanwhile, junior stared into my eyes while he slowly licked the spices from his lips. I wanted to hop across the picnic table and lick them off myself.

Instead, I looked away and drank another beer. This trip was going to be more of a challenge than I had originally expected. All I could think about was how much I wanted Mojito. And apparently, I was in his wet dreams as well.

By nightfall we'd crossed the border into North Carolina. I was driving so I pulled off the highway to look for a motel for the night. We'd head to Duke University in the morning and wander around Durham, check out the school and the city. But we wouldn't make it there that night. We were all hungry, tired, stiff from hours spent sitting, and the kind of punchy one becomes during long boring car trips.

I drove past a string of neon-lit motels that did not look inviting. Finally, Mr. Mojito told me to pull in at a brightly lit Sheraton, so I did. I parked in a dark spot at the rear of the lot and we all piled out of the car. There were only a few other cars in the parking area.

"I'll see if they have any vacancies tonight," Mr. Mojito joked.

While he booked us two rooms, Mojito and I stood together by the car, which was still ticking and hot to the touch. I felt the same way. The two of us laughed as we were both stretching our limbs and groaning.

He said, "So are you bunking with me or the old man?"

My heart surged into my throat and caught there. But when I looked in his eyes, I could see he was only joking.

"Very funny," I said with a disappointed grin. "I guess I

should wait until your father and I are married to share his hotel room, but I'm not that type of woman."

It was cold out and there was a harsh wind, but I was sweating. I stretched my arms over my head and closed my eyes.

Suddenly, Mojito was on me. He had his hands on my shoulders as he pushed me against the side of the Cadillac. He thrust a knee in my crotch, held it there. Like he wanted to make sure I couldn't escape.

But I wasn't going anywhere.

"I have no doubt about that, Dr. O," he said in a gruff voice. Then he kissed me. Hard.

My legs gave way and I started to slide down toward the asphalt. Mojito lifted me up by the armpits. Staring in my eyes, he ran a slow hand across my right breast. Then my left.

I would have taken him right there, I was incapable of controlling myself at that point. My heart raced and my limbs were like jelly. All I could think was Mojito, my Mojito.

Fortunately, his father chose that moment to reappear, hotel key cards in hand. "What the hell?"

Mojito yanked me to his side, holding me up with both hands. "She almost fainted, Dad. We better get her to the room."

I played along, although I was pretty weak at that point so it wasn't much of a stretch. The two men assisted me into the bright white lobby and across the white-tiled room into a glistening elevator. While we rode up to the sixth floor, I leaned against Mr. Mojito. But his son slid a sneaky hand behind us and cupped my ass cheek, the little devil.

We headed down the carpeted hall together, me protesting I was "fine" and could make it on my own, thank you, them propping me up between them. When we stood outside the room, junior ran a stimulating finger down my spine while his father fiddled with the key card. It was all I could do not to slap his hand away, or lunge for him. He was teasing me and we both loved it.

Of course I pretended nothing was going on and remained on track with my plan. My lust was overruled by the solidity of my long-term goals. I may be a sexual deviant but I'm not stupid. Or I wasn't stupid yet. That would come later.

Mr. Mojito sat me on the queen bed and undressed me gently. I lay down and he left me alone to drift into an exhausted but overstimulated sleep.

When he woke me later with his semi-magical penis, I kept my eyes closed and, well, you can imagine what I fantasized about.

I wondered if Mojito was awake in the adjoining room, whether he could hear his father's grunting, his quick but enthusiastic release.

T he room was dark when I opened my eyes. 6am and I felt fully rested, so I got out of bed quietly and headed for the bathroom, where I took a long hot shower. Under the heavy spray, I vowed to keep my heart's true love at a greater distance, both physically and in my imagination. After all, the goal of this trip was to exhibit my innate skill at creating family bonds for the father while increasing the son's pent-up desire for me. It was a balancing act, and I couldn't blow it with my adolescent lust. Or my lust for adolescents.

In the steamy bathroom, I slathered my dry skin with coconut lotion and doctored my eye bags with cover-up. The mirror was being unkind that morning. What I needed was a boozy pick-me-up, but that wouldn't happen on this trip either. A few beers was okay, getting drunk would be dangerous. Again I vowed to exert the utmost self-control.

How little we know ourselves, eh?

Mr. Mojito was up and dressed in slacks and a tangerine polo shirt when I emerged from the bathroom. He said, "I'll go grab us some coffee and we can get an early start. I already texted the kid so he's ready to head out too."

He kissed me lightly on the lips, then left me to my packing.

When I stepped out of the lobby and carried my suitcase over to the car, the boys were standing there in the early morning air, which was cold and sweet. The birds were singing and the sun was lighting up the royal blue sky. Mojito looked so young, his hair slick from the shower, his sweater a pastel peach number you'd wear on a golf course. He helped me put my suitcase in the back but said nothing.

Mojito drove and I spread out in the spacious backseat. I sipped the tepid coffee as we eased back onto the highway. Mr. Mojito chattered but his son was silent. Occasionally our eyes would meet in the rearview mirror but I made myself look away each time it happened.

The road was nearly empty and Mojito drove fast. We were only a few hours from Durham, so I told them everything I knew about Duke University. There was the prestige all graduates were privy to, and the worldwide network of Duke grads who helped each other score the best positions in the best companies. The Duke basketball team was always tops. And the campus was gorgeous, green and hilly with ivy-covered buildings that looked like Hogwarts from Harry Potter.

Mojito didn't say anything but his father asked a lot of questions and seemed interested in the school. He might have to donate very generously to the Duke legacy fund to ensure his kid got in, but he had the money so why not? He'd have to do the same at Princeton, Columbia, and Harvard too. Legacy, as it was known back then. Before the cheating elites got busted for paying their kids' way into the top colleges.

Mojito would like Duke, I was sure of it. But I doubted he would have a say in the matter. He'd go to the college where Dad sent him. And Dad wanted the best of the best of everything. Dad wanted the Ivy Leagues.

We pulled into Durham at lunchtime and Mojito parked the Escalade in a small but busy downtown area not far from campus. The boys wanted meat again so we found an upscale burger bistro and sat on stools at the mahogany bar. I ordered a garden salad and lusted after the rows of sparkling liquor bottles lined up against the mirrored wall. Drinks made with a vanilla-flavored tequila were on special. But it was barely noon and I was playing the role of proud mom with her college-bound offspring, so I nibbled at my romaine and pretended to be content.

This "fun" road trip was turning out to be long hours of boredom, ruined further by the need to fake it constantly while secretly lusting after what my heart and soul really craved. But what had I expected? The wanting and not having? That was the story of my life.

"You seem quiet today," Mr. Mojito said, wiping burger juice from his stubbled chin. "You feel okay?"

His tan was already fading and he looked kind of yellow under the bar lights. And old, he looked old.

I managed a smile. "I'm fine." I'd never been to Duke before, but I'd gone online to do the necessary research. "We must spend time in the flower garden. It's supposed to be truly amazing."

After lunch we parked at the visitors' lot on campus and joined a prospective student tour. The dining halls were modern, full of chatting students who looked well kept and, well, wealthy. The ceiling of the basketball auditorium held dozens of banners illustrating Duke's years of winning seasons. The dorms were like New York brownstones with an eighteenth-century European flair. The tennis courts were state of the art.

We left the tour to spend time in the flower garden. The online information did not do the botanical garden justice. It was too early in the season for some of the flowers to be in bloom, but everything was green and jungle lush. The cool afternoon air smelled delightful.

"I could be happy here," Mojito told me after we ended up side by side a few paces ahead of his father.

"If I were here with you, perhaps," I teased.

He snorted. "You think you have some kind of sexual power over me, don't you," he said in a voice so low I could barely hear it.

"I *know* I do," I responded, then walked ahead, making sure to move my shapely ass with just enough twang.

We were on the road again, discussing the pros and cons of Duke. There weren't any cons, not that I could see. Oh, Duke wasn't one of the eight Ivies, but most of the world considered it one. Still, Mr. Mojito had his reservations.

"The parking seems tough, really tight," Mr. Mojito commented. "And the downtown area is so small. Not much choice in shopping and dining. Not sure the town has much to offer you, son."

Such a snob.

I countered with, "Who cares? He'll be on campus most of the time and won't need a car. Kids Uber everywhere now, which is safer when they're partying anyway."

Mojito looked over his shoulder to give me a half smile and a thumbs up.

"I love that school, personally," I added. "I'd be over the moon if I had a teaching job there." Flirting with Duke undergrads?

Heavenly! "Some of my favorite authors are Duke grads." When they didn't ask who, I listed them anyway. "Anne Tyler, William Styron, Dan Mallory, David Brooks..."

Neither of my boys was listening so I dropped the subject and asked if we would make it to Princeton in time for dinner.

"It's maybe seven hours if we don't get boxed in on the beltway around D.C.," Mr. Mojito answered.

Then he turned on the radio and found a satellite broadcast of some stupid hockey game. The boys were thrilled.

Yawn.

I tuned out and stared out the window, admiring the North Carolina flora. Unlike the sparse palm-lined streets of South Florida, here the neighborhoods were shaded by old growth trees thick with greenery. I wasn't lying (for once) when I said I'd love to teach in a town like this. Of course, I'd never qualify for that kind of job, not with my sketchy resume. Phony Florida where everyone's a con was about the best I could hope for in the career department. But I knew I didn't have anyone to blame for that except myself.

I closed my eyes, let my head loll. The men listened to the game and I zoned out. I would have to have a few drinks before dinner. The boredom had become intolerable for someone not used to such long stretches of sobriety.

Even after we were back on the interstate heading into Virginia, the hockey game continued. That shit just went on and on. My boys talked easily, comparing notes on various players and their stats. Eventually I nodded off. I wasn't tired, but I felt ignored. After this, I decided, I wouldn't sit in the back of the car anymore, no matter how comfortable it was. I needed their eyes on me, not on each other.

I woke up with drool on my face and the setting sun in my eyes.

We were off the highway, parked at a service station. Mojito was pumping gas and his dad was nowhere in sight.

After I wiped off my chin and fluffed my matted hair, I rolled out of the car. The one-lane road we'd come in on was empty of cars. We were the only ones at the pumps. Inside the glass-front service station, I could see the clerk's dreads and the TV over his upturned head. The store was empty of customers. There was nobody else around.

Crickets chirped from the tall pines surrounding the service station. Otherwise, the evening was oddly quiet.

"Where are we?" I asked Mojito, who was ignoring me.

He didn't look up but continued filling the tank. The car was a beast and a gas guzzler, but I was half in love with it. Nobody messes with you on the highway when you barrel up in an Escalade. You're in the captain's seat.

"Not far from Princeton. My dad wants to get there tonight. I think he has someplace in mind for us to get a late dinner." His voice was subdued.

"Are you okay? Something wrong?"

He removed the nozzle from the tank and, finally, looked over at me. "Are you serious, lady?" His beautiful eyes were clouded over, like the ocean before a storm. "I'm looking at colleges with my elitist dad who doesn't like the parking situation at Duke, and my slut teacher who is trying her best to make me go insane. So, no, I'm not fucking okay. Okay?" His voice was a sneer, and he turned his back on me to deal with the pump.

I walked around the rear of the car and slid into the driver's seat. When he glanced in through the window, I gave him the finger. To my surprise, he laughed.

Mr. Mojito walked up with a six-pack of Heineken. "Oh, you're driving now, Cathriona? No beer for you then, young lady."

I gave him the finger and he laughed too.

The men piled in and I roared out of the gas station. I was really pissed off. They thought I was kidding but I was angry with both of them. They'd drink beer and talk hockey while I suffered in silence.

Fuck men. You can't live with them, you can't kill them. Or can you? I was tempted.

This wouldn't be the last time I felt that way. Oh no, it sure wouldn't.

11

The little township of Princeton was like something out of a European fairytale. Pristine multi-acre estates boasting budding maple trees, rustic stone walls, and long majestic driveways. Huge white colonials and red-brick mansions set back on steep green inclines overlooking the narrow streets. Pretty, preppy-looking people in pastels walking casually along airbrushed sidewalks. Cozy cafés with striped awnings, dusty antique shops next to upscale stores selling fancy pet supplies and overpriced hardware. Even the streetlights were classy.

I gawked at everything as we drove by, admiring the contented-looking elite and their quaint little town. This was a place I could get used to.

Following Mr. Mojito's directions, I parked in a small lot behind a classic stone building that would have been at home in a village in the Italian Alps. Mr. Mojito said the place was called Pasta Fiesta. Mojito read from his phone: "Family-style Italian food served in a formal setting. Outdoor seating, weather permitting."

He laughed. It was maybe only fifty degrees out. In Florida, weather permitting meant year-round unless there was a hurricane.

"I don't think I'm dressed for this place," I worried. My black tights were bagging at the knees and I'd put on a bulky cable-knit sweater once the sun went down. I looked like a hitchhiker, not a preppy wife. "Should we maybe find a hotel first?"

Mr. Mojito reached over to put a reassuring hand on my thigh. "I have connections here, so no worries. This place has rooms upstairs. If I get my way, and I usually do, we can stay here tonight. I just need to talk to the right people. And the food here is top-notch. So we'll have a late dinner and see what I can do."

I smiled at him. That sounded good to me. I was pretty sure they'd have a well-stocked bar too. So maybe I could have a drink or three.

I slid out of the driver's seat and followed the men across the parking lot. Mojito held the door for his father and me. When I pushed by Mojito, his elbow lightly brushed against my right breast. I snickered under my breath.

My boy was bad, bad, bad.

The restaurant was lovely inside, candlelit and white table-clothed with the rich aroma of garlic bread emanating from the kitchen. The maître d' greeted Mr. Mojito like an old friend with big hugs and kisses on both cheeks. After we were introduced to the friendly Alberto, he led us to a table for four by the front window. Mojito and I sat across from each other. Mr. Mojito remained standing and spoke to Alberto in a hushed voice while Mojito and I avoided each other's eyes.

I stared at the bar. Well stocked indeed.

Mr. Mojito sat beside me and leaned in. "There's a room available upstairs if you want to freshen up before dinner."

I did. But I wanted a drink first.

"Will we be staying here tonight?" I asked.

He said yes just as an elderly waitress with steel gray hair arrived with a bottle of Tuscan red and two glasses.

"Would it be appropriate to take a glass of wine up to our room while I change?" I asked Mr. Mojito.

He told me to stay put, to relax and enjoy the wine. Then he nodded to Mojito and they left me there with the bottle of red while they went out to the car to retrieve our baggage and bring it upstairs.

I sucked down the first glass, then quickly poured myself another. I was finishing that one when Mr. Mojito returned sans son. He sat down beside me and reached for the bottle, pouring us each a glass.

"Go ahead up if you want. Room 2. Your suitcase is by the bed." He reached for my hand and kissed my palm while staring into my eyes with puppy dog loyalty, trust, and love. Poor man.

I stood, picking up my full glass. But before I left, I leaned down to kiss the top of his head. Mr. Mojito was such a nice man. He deserved better than me.

Most men did.

Wine glass in hand, I headed up the thickly carpeted stairs to the rooms on the second floor. The long hallway was dark and quiet. Oil paintings of the Italian countryside dotted the walls. Goats and milkmaids, wine grapes and Chianti bottles in straw baskets. Room 2 was at the far end of the hall. I wondered if Mojito was in room 1 across the way. I stood by that door and pressed my ear to the burnished wood. I heard nothing.

When I realized I didn't have a key to room 2, I thought I would have to go back downstairs. I stood outside the room for a moment and sipped my wine. Then I tried the old-fashioned glass doorknob, and it turned easily. I guess theft at this place was not a threat, which made me wonder who owned the business. We were in Jersey after all, home of the *Sopranos* and real-life mobsters.

The room was softly carpeted, warm, and surprisingly spacious. It was more like a suite, with a formal sitting area featuring a rose-hued wingback chair and a long matching couch. Conveniently stationed by the glass coffee table was a wheeled bar cart.

Bingo.

Polishing off the wine left in my glass, I went straight to the bar cart and scanned until I spotted a bottle of tequila. I would do a couple shots of Gold before returning to the restaurant. I set my wine glass on the coffee table and headed to the door to the bedroom. Dress up then load up.

I opened the bedroom door and walked inside the dark room, scanning the floor for my suitcase while mentally planning what I would wear to dinner. My little black dress with the buttons up the front, my cherry-red Jimmy Choo heels. I'd put my hair up and...

I nearly fainted when he spoke. I jumped and he laughed at me.

I hadn't noticed him lying on the bed. His zipper was down and he had his dick in his hand.

"See what you do to me?" he said.

That's when I saw my panties, the ones with the pink hearts on them. They were lying on the pillow by his head. Had he been sniffing them?

Men. Such animals!

I walked over to the bed, which was king sized and covered in thick colorful quilts. He was as well hung as I'd expected, and sure to pack even more punch than the old man. But there was no way I was going to join in any of his reindeer games. Not yet anyway.

"Are you out of your mind?" I asked in a low voice, looming over him. "What if it had been your father who walked in here?"

He stroked himself. "He said you were coming up to change.

I couldn't help it. I heard you two last night and since I'm going to be right over there on the couch tonight, I'll have to listen all over again."

This was crazy. He was sleeping on the couch? All of us, all night, in the same hotel suite?

He stared at me, his eyes like superhero magnets. I could feel him drawing me into his lust orbit. My crotch dampened.

He moaned theatrically. "You're killing me, Dr. O, you know that."

Was I?

I leaned over and grabbed his hard cock, held it in my hand. His skin was baby soft. He closed his eyes and gave himself to me.

It only took a minute and he was done.

"You better make sure there's nothing on the bedspread," I said as I sashayed to the bathroom.

Closing the door behind me, I stripped off my travel clothes and hopped in the shower, hoping he would show up and join me. I was also hoping he wouldn't. He didn't, so I stepped out and toweled off. I braided my hair and wrapped it around itself so that it stayed up on my head.

Dressed only in the fluffy red towel, I returned to the bedroom and busied myself in my already opened suitcase. Mojito still lay on the bed with his zipper down, and his cock was hard again. Oh, the joys of youth! He was ready to go at it and I couldn't, I shouldn't, I wouldn't.

Oh, but I wanted to.

"Come here," he said in a quiet but demanding voice.

I walked over to him and leaned down so our noses were touching. His eyes glistened and he smelled like fresh cut wood and Red Delicious apples. He slid one cool hand inside the towel and pinched my nipples until they hardened, then licked the shower water from my neck.

After I reached for the panties that lay on the pillow beside his head, I stood upright again, holding the towel closed with one hand. "I'm going to dress for dinner. You can watch," I said. "After all, we're practically family. Right?"

He snorted but didn't object.

I dropped the towel to the floor and made a big show of bending over and stepping into my panties. No bra for tonight, I played with my breasts then pulled on the black dress. I buttoned myself up very slowly. I knew how to do the reverse stripper act. Men loved it.

Boys did too.

I perched on the foot of the bed to pull on a pair of sheer black hose. He watched me silently, then I heard him working it.

Live porno starring Dr. O? Live porno starring future step-mom? Ick.

"This little game we played? Make sure it's just between us," I told him without looking over. I stood and put on my five-inch designer heels. I towered over the bed, staring down and locking eyes, glaring at him. "Nobody will ever know we did this. Understand?"

He didn't say anything. His face was so young. So disappointed.

I turned to go but before I was out the door, he said, "This isn't over, *Stepmom*. I want to be inside you and you want me there. This was just foreplay."

I glanced over my shoulder. He had his pants zipped up and was wiping off the bedspread with the bath towel.

"So you say," I said. "But that's not necessarily what *I* have in mind."

I left, stopping only to fill my wine glass with two fingers of tequila.

By the time I got downstairs, I was nice and toasted.

12

Dinner was a blur because I ordered a chocolate martini and that pushed me over the edge. I think I ordered eggplant rollatini, but I'm not sure. Mojito didn't join us, so I let his father blather on and on over the four-course meal while I got seriously plastered. He had to practically carry me up the stairs and pour me into bed, which I believe he enjoyed. When I was drunk, he could just fuck me, he didn't need to woo me or seduce me or please me.

What man doesn't enjoy that?

While he plowed his way inside me, I kept my eyes closed. I imagined it was my boy with his baby soft skin, his ever-hard dick, his beseeching eyes. Oh Mojito, you think *I'm* killing *you*? This is a two-way street, baby, and we're both driving way over the speed limit.

I guessed Mojito had found a bar to hang out in because he didn't come back to the room until much later. I woke when I heard him stumbling around the living area, then collapsing on the couch. I had a massive headache so I got up to take a couple of Advils. Mr. Mojito was snoring. The man could sleep.

Yes, I could've used the bathroom sink to grab some water to wash down the pills, but I chose instead to wander out to the sitting room in search of bottled water. I found it on the bar cart. How convenient.

Of course, my boy sat up at once.

I popped two blue gel pills and handed him two more. After I swigged some water, I passed him the bottle.

"Preventive medicine," I said. "Where've you been?"

"Out. With the young folks," he said, avoiding my eyes.

How mean.

"Okay, baby, I get it. You're mad at Mommy because she wouldn't put out. Get over it," I said very quietly. I snatched the water bottle from his hands, and went back to his dad.

Unfortunately, I was unable to fall back to sleep for an annoyingly long time. So when the morning sun crept in around the damask curtains, it felt like I had just dozed off.

Mr. Mojito woke me up with a cup of hot coffee and a kiss on the nose. "Let's go, sleepyhead. College tour starts at nine."

I sat up gingerly but my head felt fine. Amazing stuff, that Advil. All I needed was a pair of sunglasses and a gallon of coffee and I would be able to make it through the morning tour of another fantastic college that would never have me as a student or teacher.

Ugh, my mood had blackened. I needed to get a grip and focus on seducing the father, not the son. Mojito was a bit of a prick and Dad was a living doll. What was wrong with me?

I brushed my teeth and undressed, then gave Mr. Mojito a very spicy good morning/thank you kiss. It wasn't difficult to lure him back into bed. We made all sorts of animal noises sure to frustrate the boy on the couch.

Touché.

Princeton University was a lot like Duke only smaller and even more elite. The tour guides were all peppy and clean scrubbed, full of helpful information and youthful zest. It made me tired just to watch them. I kept my shades on inside the ivy-covered halls, the expansive auditoriums and lecture halls, the modern dorms and dining areas. Mojito did too. I would've laughed with him at our shared hungover state, but he acted as if I didn't exist. If I spoke, he pretended not to hear me.

When his father took me to lunch at a fancy bistro in Palmer Square, Mojito said he wanted to get a smoothie instead and wandered off.

"What's with him today?" Mr. Mojito asked, setting down the menu.

I grunted my ignorance, keeping a menu in front of my face. I was embarrassed. I'd behaved badly, although most of the blame could be put on Mojito. He'd started it, lying in wait for me like that, in the dark on our bed with his pants open. I reassured myself that it was not my fault, then set down my menu.

"I'm going to have the onion soup," I said with a phony smile. "And a small glass of rosé."

An hour later, when we reconnoitered in the room at the restaurant hotel, Mojito said he didn't want to visit Columbia and Harvard. "I've kind of had it with the Ivies, Dad," he explained. "Can we save New York and Boston for later? I met a girl last night and I'd kind of like to stick around here for another few days, see her again, take her out to dinner or something. I can fly home after. You guys can keep going. To the mountains or whatever."

He avoided my eyes. Good thing too because I was furious.

He had a *girl*? He'd met some chick last *night*? After fooling around with *me*?

I sat on the couch and buried my head in an orange-and-black-striped Princeton alumni magazine so they couldn't see my hot angry face. The little shit!

But it was the most the kid had said all day, so his father was relieved. Although he was not on board with the idea. "You can fly home from Newark today if you want, but you can't hang around Princeton on your own. You aren't even eighteen yet, son. You're still my responsibility."

Mojito frowned in disappointment, but he nodded his acquiescence.

His father continued, "We could skip the colleges and head straight for Vermont. You must want to see the green mountain state?"

Mojito shook his head. "Nah. But can we stay here one more night? I'd really like to see Brandi again."

Mr. Mojito looked at me. What could I say? I fake grinned, shrugged. So we'd stay another night. So what?

There was always the bar cart.

Mr. Mojito said he would go downstairs to talk to management.

"Maybe you can get him his own room for tonight," I suggested as Mr. Mojito headed for the door. "That couch won't fit two."

My way of pretending I wasn't jealous.

Mojito gave me a strange look, but his father said, "Good idea."

After he shut the door behind him, I put down the alumni magazine and stood. I went over to the bar cart and poured two shots of Gold. Handing one to Mojito, I said, "Hair of the dog's tail that wagged you last night. Cheers."

We shot them down.

He smiled a little at me, warming up again. So I said, "Listen, we need to get along, you and me. You need to make an effort for your father's sake. That man has done everything for you."

Mojito looked away. "You're right. He's a really good guy." His voice sharpened then and he stared at me. "But you? You're like me, you have an empty place for a soul." He ran his eyes over my body and I shivered. "But maybe that's what he likes about you. I can see why, so I'll just let him have his fun. Like you say, I'll be cool and back off."

I poured us two more shots but he shook his head. "I want to be sober for this date tonight. She's a nice girl."

As opposed to me, a dirty old lady, I thought. A slut. A whore well past her sell-by date. Ugh.

I pounded the shot, then walked to the bedroom. If he'd followed me in, God knows, I probably would've fucked him. That's how weak he made me.

Mojito. Oh, Mojito.

13

We ended up staying in Princeton for three more nights. In the same restaurant hotel, but in separate suites. It was intolerable. I could barely keep my skin on, I was crawling out of it day and night. But Mr. Mojito was happy the kid was on his own, and I played real hard at being the contented fiancée. We took chilly walks around the area townships, drove out to the local malls, ate lots of fancy meals, had lots of dull sex. I drank too much. But I always drink too much.

Soon enough, it was time to fly home to Florida.

So much for hiking in the mountains. Not that I wanted to, but I was kind of dismayed that our east coast trip had ended in Jersey. But Mr. Mojito seemed to have quite a bit of business in the area. He left me at the Lawrenceville shopping malls for hours at a time while he "visited some business associates." What was that about? Had he planned this or was it a coincidence? Or was he just taking advantage of us being stuck in Princeton while his son wooed some nineteen-year-old barmaid?

I asked no questions. Oh no. I was the perfect fiancée, the kind who would make the perfect wife. Yes, yes, yes.

We turned in the rental car and flew home on Thursday night. Mojito seemed sad to leave his new squeeze, and he kept to himself. He avoided flirting with me, which I both appreciated and resented.

Fort Lauderdale International Airport was a mental asylum and the traffic on I-95 homicidal, but I was happy to be back in the blazing sunlight, listening to the gentle sound of the ocean waves, basking in the solitude of my condo. I took the weekend off from men, alcohol, and talking. Instead, I wrote and slept, and I felt more like myself than I had in a long time.

On Sunday night I prepared a fresh avocado mask and popped a vegan pizza in the microwave. I had just stretched myself across the couch with Zora curled up by my feet. We were about to watch a Lifetime full-Kleenex-box girlie movie when the buzzer went. A visitor? Who would visit me now, at nine o'clock on a Sunday night?

I sighed loudly and shifted my feet. The cat gave me the hairy eyeball. She didn't want visitors either. "Don't blame me," I told her. "Let's ignore them, shall we."

Zora closed her eyes.

Then I got a text.

"Sorry, Z," I said and she leaped to the floor, disappearing down the hall when I jumped up. I buzzed my surprise guest inside the building.

By the time he knocked on my door, the avocado was off my face and my hair was down and brushed, a light gloss of lipstick on my lips. I opened the door and grabbed his forearm, yanking him inside.

"You can't come here. Are you crazy? I'm your teacher, I could get fired."

He looked down at me for a moment. I felt small, fragile, vulnerable, and I liked that, I felt it in my deepest parts.

"You can't stay," I said. "What do you want?"

His eyes were red and watery.

"Are you high?" I asked.

He shook his head. "The girl from Princeton? She broke up with me."

My heart lifted. "I'm sorry, baby. Come in and sit down. I'll get you a Coke."

He followed me into the living room. When Pearl scooted by him to take cover in the bedroom, he smiled.

I fixed us a couple of Cokes on ice, adding a dash of vodka to mine. I brought the drinks out on a tray, along with a chunk of Brie and some wheat crackers. After setting the tray on the coffee table, I picked up my glass and sat at the far end of the couch, my feet tucked under me. His head was down and he stared at the floor, ignoring the snack tray.

My drink was strong. I might have overpoured.

"You wanna talk about it?" I asked him.

Of course he did or he wouldn't have come by.

He shrugged, didn't look up.

After a minute, he muttered, "I liked her. We texted a lot, talked on the phone for hours, I thought we connected. She's not intellectual at all but she's wise, street smart. I would've applied to Princeton to be near her if it worked out. But she texted me a few hours ago and said she wanted to move on. I'm 'too young', she needs a 'grown man'." He used finger quotes, scowling at me. "All you bitches are the same. You got no use for us young men who can do you right."

I snickered at his slang. "Uh, you might not want to compare your middle-aged English teacher with a nineteen-year-old waitress."

His turn to laugh. "Brandi isn't nineteen. I lied so Dad wouldn't flip out. She's around thirty, I think, a single mom with a kid in middle school. She works at the hotel in the back office."

I was stunned. So I wasn't the only cougar who went for

Mojito. For some reason, this information infuriated me and reassured me at the same time. It also made me horny.

Or maybe that was the vodka. Whatever it was, I instantly lost control.

I stood and undid the knot at the waist of my sweat shorts. Then I let them drop to the floor. He stared at me, his eyes large and full of surprise.

"One way to get over a breakup is to have sex with someone else," I said, my voice hoarse. I ran my hand over my breasts, and down my hips to my crotch.

He slid down the couch until he was within reach, then he reached for me. I was wet, and he quickly pushed aside the crotch of my white panties and inserted a finger into the dampness. I moaned and slid to the floor and he was on top of me and we were kissing, our tongues deep in each other's throats.

I pulled away, panting, trying to catch my breath.

He said, "That was helpful. But now I need the full cure."

Funny boy.

I stood and took him by the hand, pulling him off the floor and leading him into my bedroom. Zora jumped off the bed and stalked out of the room. Mojito and I looked at each other and laughed.

"I knew you had cats," he said.

"So?" I undid the zipper on his jeans.

He pulled his T-shirt over his head and stepped out of his pants. "Don't all writers have cats?"

I laughed but he was probably half right. I *was* the type to house a hundred feral cats amongst stacks of old newspapers, yellowed books and moldy fruit. Maybe litters of baby mice too. You know, that crazy writer lady who lives in filth.

Suddenly, my mood shifted and I stepped away. "You better go. You can't be here. We can't be doing this."

I started to walk out of the room but he grabbed my hand and pulled me to him. "Shut up, Dr. O."

Then he kissed me like no man had ever kissed me before.

After we pulled apart, both of us were damp with lust and shaking with desire. Without looking at me, he put on his clothes and left.

Oh, Mojito. What was I supposed to do with you?

14

One morning several months later, I woke up to the peaceful sounds of gulls calling and waves washing the sand. The salt air that eased in my open bedroom window smelled fresh and clean. But when I sat up, I felt sick. Not from drinking. From awakening to the mess I'd made of my life.

Sinking back against the pillows, I quelled the nausea by counting the days in my head. Forty-two days to the big event. Damn.

We were planning a mid-summer wedding. Casual but elegant, expensive. We'd get married at the house in a private ceremony. Then we'd party with friends. Good food, good wine, a band out on the lawn. After that, a cruise to Alaska, followed by a month at a villa in Tuscany. I'd never been either place, and both appealed. I should have been elated. Especially because, after the summer's delightful travels, I would not have to return to teaching. Not unless I chose to.

The key word being *chose*. My husband-to-be was leaving that decision up to me.

I yawned, rubbed my eyes. I had the life, right?

So why did I want to pull the covers back over my head and

sleep my future away? Why in God's name was I dismally bleak, my eyes dried out from weeping? Wasn't it every woman's dream to marry a rich, handsome, kind man? On a beautiful summer day? On the expansive grounds of a magnificent estate that would become her new home? Didn't all women wish to be whisked away by an adoring partner, disappearing on a glamorous honeymoon, bound for some of the most romantic places in the world?

Yes, of course. But those were other women's dreams. My dream was to run off with my fiancé's teenage son. To escape my sham life for the reality of my deepest passion. To spend the remainder of my sorry life with the boy I loved.

But that would never happen. Why, you ask? Ladies and gents, may I present exhibit C: baby on board.

Yes, I was pregnant with his child. Whose child, you ask? That was the million-dollar question, yes. Father's? Son's? Sadly, there was no way to tell.

I lay on my back, allowing the day's first tears to leak from my eyes. Every morning when I woke to face the new day, I wept. The crying would not stop, tears seeping down my face to soak my pillows. Nobody kissed them away. No one even heard my sobs.

Even though I had two lovers, or perhaps because of that, I felt more alone than ever.

My insane little soap opera had escalated since the premature engagement announcement out on the dock. More time had passed since the road trip and Mojito's first visit to my condo. Somehow, events had managed to well up to a painful peak, then cascade down around us, creating a bit of a bloody avalanche. Eventually, everything slid downhill. As everything in life eventually does. But really, the beginning of the end had already arrived the moment Mojito found out I was sleeping with his hero.

For that had been his attitude toward his father. At least until I came along and ruined their relationship. From what I could tell, Mojito had worshipped his dad. And Mr. Mojito was proud and supportive of his only son. Abandoned together by the same woman, the two males had formed a solid team. It had been the Mojito boys against the world.

Until Dr. Cathriona O'Hale appeared. Now it was father against son, son against father. And me playing both ends against the middle. With a slowly expanding middle of my own that neither man knew anything about.

I pulled the sheets up over my head and tried to will myself back into dreamland. But my sobs drove the sleep away. I could not escape. I was stuck in funhouse mirror world. And it was turning out to be more of a nightmare than I ever imagined.

A flock of parrots flew down the beach, squawking wildly. I wanted to join them, fly away. To where? Anywhere but here. Far away from the drama I had created.

But I didn't have that option. Wherever I went, there I would be. Me, old and pregnant. Ugh.

With a choked sigh, I got out of bed and dragged myself to the bathroom. I had time. It was still dark, way too early to head for school. After carefully examining my swollen eyes and the dark circles underneath them in the mirror over the sink, I turned to check on my profile.

And there it was. The telltale baby bump.

Damn.

I ran the shower and let the water heat up while I brushed the bitter taste of vomit from my mouth. Either I had an all-day case of morning sickness or the emotional rollercoaster of my situation was making me ill. I tossed meals on a regular basis and sometimes the only thing I could keep down was a medicinal glass or two (or three) of something strong.

I know, I know. I'm not ignorant. I was well aware I shouldn't consume alcohol now that I was, apparently, pregnant. But how would I explain myself to my lovers, both of whom were used to my party-hardy ways? I was not ready to be outed. I needed to be sure of my path forward first. Then I would make my grand announcement.

My out-of-control body trembled while I soaped and rinsed off. The hot water eased the cramped muscles in my neck, back, and legs. I wished it would ease my tense mind as well. There had to be a way out of my conundrum. But my rocketing hormones were interfering with my normal sharpness. I couldn't see things clearly. I was thinking inside a box inside the box. I was trapped in there. No exit.

While I toweled off, my phone pinged. A text from my lover.

Tonight, it said. *He's not back until ten.*

My heart lifted. Mojito. Mo-hee-toe.

My place, I texted back. *Seven.*

OK.

And like that, as if by magic or universal decree, I felt better. More energetic and lighthearted than I had been in days. In the steam-fogged mirror, my smiling face looked like my own again. When I rolled on some peachy lipstick and fluttered my lashes, I realized I hadn't managed to muster up a real smile in a long while. Not since the last time my young stud had booked a date with me.

Only Mojito made me happy. Everything else in my life was just there to hold me back. From my future. My dream. My love. When we were alone, a world of beauty and peace existed for me. And that was where I belonged, in that world, in his arms.

Sighing deeply, I lost the smile. There were so many obstacles to that shade of paradise. My life was littered with obstacles to being with Mojito.

I managed to swallow two pieces of dry toast, washed down with a cup of milky tea. After I poured some dry food for the cats, I organized the day's lesson plans and wrote for a while. When it was time, I headed for school.

The morning had turned wet, the sky heavy, threatening. Thick gray clouds stampeded overhead. Traffic moved slowly through the flooded streets. Florida's sprawling cities had been stupidly designed for a desert environment. There was nowhere for all that rain to go.

While I sat through endless delays, only to inch forward to the next in a string of exasperatingly long red lights, I thought about what had happened to my life. How it had been wrenched out of my hands. How I had given up control over my feelings, my emotions, my real self. Willingly.

To a seventeen-year-old.

After the night I pushed him away upon leading him into my bedroom, Mojito had basically ignored me. In class, in the halls at school, at the Mojitos' house, whenever we happened to be in the same vicinity. Oh, he was polite. But he looked right through me. I had become invisible to him. Just some older woman of no interest to a beautiful young guy like Mojito.

When I got wind that he had a new girlfriend, I snooped around at school to find out who she was. It didn't take me long; their PDAs were splashed up and down the school halls and all over social media. Greta Cantoli, a slim dark beauty from upscale Boca Raton. Her family hailed from New Jersey, where they'd been in construction, and they appeared to have mountains of new money. Mojito really seemed to like those Jersey girls.

I knew who she was. The girl was too thin, in my opinion, and she dressed sort of cheesy. But what she lacked in class she made up for in sex appeal. Innocently slutty, she had that busty spoiled pout the boys all liked. I think she ran with a fast crowd. She dressed like a hooker, wore lots of kohl around her wide green eyes. I watched her in the parking lot, leaning against him and laughing.

Marking her territory. Marking my Mojito.

The pain was unbearable. I agonized, enough that Mojito's father eventually noticed my demoralized bearing. He asked if I felt ill, then worried aloud he'd done something wrong. Poor Mr. Mojito. Always trying to take care of those who wanted only to take from him. He was too good for me.

At least, that's what I thought at the time.

One night I was at the house waiting for Mr. Mojito to return from a business trip. He'd been gone a full week and I'd actually missed him. He was, I told myself, a giving lover and a good conversationalist. So what if he failed to ignite that special spark? While he was out of town, I had almost convinced myself to accept the gift I'd been offered, to lie back and enjoy it. After all, I wasn't getting any younger. My looks were failing me, and the end result would not be pretty. This kind of matrimonial opportunity would not come my way again. As the wife of a rich man, I could relax into the slothful lifestyle I preferred. Write at my leisure, maybe even buy myself a book contract with a major publisher. Life could be good.

Besides, I was starting to believe the horrid truth: I might never have my way with Mojito. The boy had his own life to lead. He had his own dreams.

That particular evening I was stretched out on a chaise longue by the pool, which was lit by an underwater lamp. A changing array of hazy colors swirled in the still water: lime green, lipstick pink, burnt tangerine, violet, and a polar blue. This was in late March, and the night was unseasonably cool. I had wool socks on my feet, a cashmere shawl wrapped around my shoulders, a drink in my hand. The stars were brilliant, blinkering in small flocks overhead. I felt relaxed, content with my decision to let go of the impossible fantasy and just be in the reality of my good fortune. I felt almost happy. Almost.

"Waiting for Dad?"

I flinched at the sound of his voice, dropping my goblet. It crashed on the pool deck, the glass shattering, expensive red wine splashing everywhere.

"Fuck, you scared me," I said, sitting up to examine the damage. The shards sparkled in the starlight, in the flickering pool light.

Mojito stood in the distance, arms folded on his chest. Tight jeans, tight long-sleeved tee, sneakers. A boy-man. He laughed at me. "I like it when you curse. I bet you don't talk like that to Dad, right?"

His voice was sneering, mean. But at least he was speaking to me like I existed. In school I got nothing out of him. In front of his father, he was polite but curt. And he never looked at me anymore. Not directly, anyway.

Tonight, he was staring right at me. Boldly, like a taunt.

He pushed further. "In bed, maybe? You two talk dirty?" He snickered at that. Like it was funny or he was an idiot.

"That's none of your business." I stood but he stepped forward, blocking my way. "Don't touch," I said in a low voice.

What I meant was, touch me.

Mojito, my love, he heard what I didn't say. He was young, but his soul was not. He must have lived other lives, long full lives of strength and power. He seemed so experienced. And intuitive. A grown man in that way.

He grabbed my shoulders, held me steady. I was trembling all over. My mouth was dry. Like I had eaten a stick of chalk. His eyes were lit up with starlight and the changing colors from the pool. I was shoeless, and the glass was all around me. I couldn't run away from him. I couldn't move.

Not that I wanted to.

"Be careful." He meant of the broken glass, but I took it another way.

"I don't want to care," I admitted.

"I know."

The only sounds after that were our breathing and the soft gurgle of the pool filter. We were frozen in place, stuck there, looking deep into one another, both deathly afraid to take the next inevitable step. That life mistake we would not be able to take back. Neither of us moved for what seemed like minutes. At one point, I felt like laughing, letting myself dissolve in a distancing fit of nervous giggles. But, my lord, the boy kept me steady with his iron grip, his chain-link gaze.

Finally, he sighed. "Oh, Cath."

When he spoke, the smell of liquor floated my way. I leaned in, sniffing. A vague scent of teenage-girl perfume, and those too-sweet alcoholic drinks. He'd been out with her and the aroma of his cheap little girlfriend still clung to his skin. I should have pulled away instantly.

Instead, for some twisted reason, this turned me on. Why should she have him to herself when I wanted him too? A primitive response, but an authentic one. I wanted, I wanted so much.

I licked my lips. Slowly.

He eased the shawl off my shoulders, methodically folding it, then dropping it on the chaise longue. When I didn't object, didn't speak, just kept my eyes on his, he continued to undress me. He unbuttoned my shirt, slid it off my shoulders and down my arms. I let it drop from my hands to the pool deck. I still hadn't moved.

We stood there in the darkness, gauging one another's desires. The tension was vibrating like a tuning fork, palpable, audible.

Vrrrrrrringgggg.

In slow motion, he reached for my breasts, unhooked the bra clasp between them. His fingers stung me with heat, with the tingle of high-wire nerves. I let the lacy thing slide off my shoulders, down my arms, and fall from my hands. He stared at my middle-aged breasts, breathing harder. I closed my eyes for a moment, praying my body excited him.

I wavered when he stepped closer to feel my backside, fondling, pressing me to him. Then he unzipped my skirt, which dropped to the pool deck. It would be wine stained when I retrieved it. So would the rest of my clothes.

He stepped away. I kept my eyes on his face, his handsome young face. I had told him I didn't want to care. But I wanted him and that was *all* I cared about.

He held back, staring, appraising me. Shivering now with apprehension as well as intense sexual excitement, I stood before him in only a skimpy pair of bikini panties and a thick pair of red socks. Black lace and Christmas stockings. The air felt cold on my naked skin. When I glanced down, the refracting pool lights flashed across my pale breasts, my soft belly and thighs. My body was a psychedelic light show.

He made a low sound then, and pressed himself against me. I let him kiss me. I let him do whatever he wanted to me. His father was due home any minute. As if thinking about this as well, Mojito kissed me hard, then harder, his mouth begging me to participate, to let go and be his. I resisted, but not for long.

When I finally kissed him back, repressed passion spilled from my mouth, my breasts, my entire body. His hot fast hands were all over me then, prodding me, thrilling me, bringing me to the edge of screaming.

I felt his arousal but when I reached for him, he grabbed my hair. Yanking my head back, he looked me in the eyes. I was panting by that time, and dripping wet.

"This what you want, Cath? Say it," he demanded.

His expression looked demented, his pretty mouth wet from me, twisted in anger or desire or both. I sucked in the cool night air, shaking uncontrollably. I didn't dare move from his grip on my shoulders, I was afraid I would slump to the deck, roll in the broken glass. The situation was ridiculous, dangerous, obscene.

"Yes," I said, licking my lips, thirsty and panting and crazed with lust. "This is what I want."

We both wanted it. So there was that, you see.

Yes. That's how it finally happened the first time. Right there, in the flashing garish neon of his mansion's pool lights. And afterward? I simply told myself it had to be. He wanted it, I wanted it. Absolutely no harm done.

But months had passed and things had changed. As I headed for another day in the classroom, sick and worried, my belly distended and my mind constantly ricocheting from this to that option, this to that scenario, I had to admit to myself that harm *had* been done. Yes, harm had indeed been done.

15

After struggling with the annoying traffic and my continuing nausea, I pulled into the school lot in a black funk. Then it got worse. Because of some event I'd been unaware of, the parking lot was full. So I drove next door and hunted down a space in the two-story garage. I hated parking in there. It was dark cornered, dank and creepy, especially on rainy days. Plus, the longer walk to class would make me late. And wet.

I locked the car and headed for the down ramp. Two school-girls sauntered toward the exit just ahead of me. They both had ear buds, so they were talking in loud voices above their loud music. I could hear every word they said.

I slowed down when I realized they were talking about him.

Mojito.

"Greta's pregnant and it's Mojito's. That's what Stacy says. It was posted last night. On Facebook." The taller stockier girl said this in a chilling delivery. Like Facebook was CNN.

The shorter one shook her head, her long red curls bouncing. Young girls have so much shine in their hair. And so much body. "Really? 'Cuz I heard he's got another girlfriend and he was breaking up with Greta. And *that's* why she slit her wrists."

What?

"Everybody knows you can't kill yourself that way," the big one sniffed. I moved close enough to hear her music. Taylor Swift? Oh please. "Guns or bridges, that's what you gotta do if you really wanna do it right."

The small one shook out that pretty hair. Flaunted it. "Yeah. But it sure got her boy's attention."

Bile inched up my throat. I'd been all excited about his early-morning text, about seeing him tonight. And apparently he had reached out to me simply because he needed some adult counseling. He must have needed input on what to do about his crazy girlfriend. Who was either suicidal, pregnant, or both. Most likely neither. Kids were notorious gossipmongers and Facebook a stirred-up pot of lies, I told myself.

But I didn't believe it.

I pushed past the dawdling girls and hurried outside. The rain was coming down in torrents.

Behind me, both girls said, "Hi, Dr. O" in monotone unison. Like a couple of cheerleaders on Valium.

I waved over my head and jogged toward the main building, my mood as sour as my stomach.

He wasn't in class.

At lunchtime, I checked the attendance lists online. He was out "sick." So was Greta. My heart joined my stomach in a pit of burning acid. I wanted to go home sick myself. But I stuck it out, teaching Hemingway and Austen to illiterates until the final bell. Then I packed up my laptop and headed for the parking garage.

The rain had stopped but the sky was still hanging low, sluggish and damp. I picked my way around the puddles and managed to stay reasonably dry. Back in the car, I sat for a moment, collecting my thoughts. And yes, they were dark. There

I was, pregnant and in love with a teenager. A seventeen-year-old boy with a teenage girlfriend in trouble. I was no more mature than Greta, apparently. And, most likely, no more beloved to Mojito.

Leaning back against the headrest, eyes closed, I swallowed the surging bile. I wanted nothing more than to strip off my work clothes, drink more than enough tequila, and pass the fuck out. The day had begun with the oblivion of sleep and that had been the high point. It had only gotten more painful after that.

My mouth was dry, my internal organs burning. I had such thirst.

By the time I started the engine, I knew what I was going to do. I would stop at the liquor store, and that night I would drink. Then the next day, after my hangover had subsided, I would make an appointment at the Planned Parenthood in Fort Lauderdale.

This was the right thing to do. In the very wrong situation I was in.

Predictably, traffic was slow, the streets still full of storm water. This gave me time to reconsider. Stop drinking? Get an abortion? Those were two options I did *not* want to take.

Crown Liquors was empty of customers and the shop reeked of cheap wine and stale sweat. Why do liquor stores all smell like unwashed drunks? Perhaps for the same reason bars smell like piss and vomit.

What would *I* smell like in the morning?

Ignoring my rising self-disgust, I wandered the bottle-lined aisles, finally selecting a nice agave tequila. The store had a small produce area where I picked up some fresh mint and a handful of limes. I would be drinking mojitos that night. With or without my date.

I avoided looking the doughy female clerk in the eye as she rang up my items. Was I imagining it, or was Fat Lady staring at my slightly bulging belly? Shame brought instant heat to my face. I ran my debit card, then rushed out of the store.

The rain had started up again with a vengeance. Oh God, oh God. What was I doing to myself?

By the time I walked in my front door, I was a wreck. Soaked, shivering, a half-drowned rodent. I headed for the bathroom, ripped off my clothes, and ran a hot bubble bath. Within seconds, the room was warm and smelled of coconut.

Standing in the kitchen naked and cold, I took the time to make myself a nice stiff drink. Sprig of mint, wedge of lime. Done. Then I made a second one. I carried both drinks into the steam-filled bathroom, where I turned off the faucets. The tub was filled to the brim and burning hot, delicious smelling.

After I stepped in carefully, I eased my body down, settling in the skin-tingling heat with a contented sigh. I closed my eyes, sipped one of my drinks, and waited for the peace of alcohol-induced oblivion to wash over me.

Instead, fleeting images invaded my mind. Mojito that night by the pool. Lifting me in his arms and carrying me to the grassy lawn. Laying me down gently, then lying on top of me. Kissing me so passionately I thought I would die. Touching me so gently I did cry. Making love to me slowly. He was tantric, this boy. Each body part was touched as if sacred. He worshipped my body, made it blush and arch, sweat and cry out, writhe and tremble. When I was spent, I wanted more. More and more.

Where had he learned to love a woman? From the hotel clerk in Princeton, perhaps? Not from brittle young Greta.

When he was deep inside me, his smell in my mouth, his hands imprinted on my skin forever, my tears on his lips, I heard something. A noise, coming from out front. We were rocking together, on the hot jagged edge of it, but he pulled out instantly. He heard it too. The sound of a purring car engine and the crunch of tires on stones in the driveway.

He sat up, listening. Both of us were still, holding our breath, alert. I recognized the familiar sound of the Rolls engine, then silence. A car door slammed.

Mojito said, "Jump in the pool. Act drunk. I'll cover for you with Father." He looked down at me, his mouth smeared from my lips, my everything. "Watch out you don't step on the glass."

He stroked my bare hip gently. Then he pulled on his clothes and jogged off.

I did what he suggested. The pool was heated, of course. In Florida, where it is summer nine or ten months of the year, all wealthy folks heat their pools anyway. Physical discomfort is simply not allowed. It's unthinkable whenever there is a solution you can purchase.

Still, the water felt like ice on my skin. I wasn't acting when I shrieked and jumped up and down in the shallow end. I wasn't faking it when I ducked under, burst up again with a scream. I was skinny dipping in "cold" weather. Florida natives don't do that. We're warm-blooded creatures.

You don't believe that about me, I know. And why would you? To you, I'm nothing but a pedophile. And a murderer. You imagine my blood must be made of dry ice.

Let me explain something to you. After that first night, after he lifted me in his arms, carried me to the soft grass and made love to me, I was madly in love with Mojito. Real love knows no age limits. Passion like that comes once in a lifetime. Or not at all. I am one of the lucky ones, you see. I have lost, yes. But I have really loved. And been loved in return.

. . .

In the warmth of my bubble-filled tub, I lay back and recalled the subsequent nights of passion, the many times he entered me, the way we came together as one being, the dusky afternoons in his boy bedroom, laughing, naked, lusting. All of that merged in my mind into one giant cloud of happiness. A white puffy cloud that was about to burst. Soaking me through my skin to my organs, through my organs to the tiny fetus afloat inside me. Poisoning it with the wrongness of our love.

The tub water was cooling when I opened my eyes. I stood and poured the second drink into the tepid bathwater.

No. Not this. There were other options. Mojito loved me, and I loved him. We would find a way to be together.

Later that night, I would fish the mint leaves and lime wedges from the empty tub. But at that moment, I needed to get dressed and brew up a pot of strong coffee. Mojito was due in less than an hour.

When seven o'clock came and went, I sat out on the patio, writing. The coffee had revived me and my body felt good. Not sick with child, but full of promise. I had just written that joyful sentiment in the context of my autobiographical story in progress, this story, when I heard a key in the lock.

Mojito.

I whipped off my glasses, slammed shut my laptop, and looked over at the door. My heart was leaping like a gymnast. Only to crash to the floor of my ribcage.

Striding across the living room: my love's father.

16

I should have known. Mojito did not have a key to my place, so it could not have been him coming through that door. But in that fraction of a second, I'd been about to say his name. And that would have been a terrible mistake. I might have ruined everything by calling out *Mojito*. The lust in my voice would've certainly betrayed me.

The thought of how easily I might have made that mistake caused me to bite my tongue. I stopped when I tasted blood.

Controlling my face, I set my glasses and my laptop on the table. "Darling? What are you doing here?" I needed to text Mojito as soon as possible and warn him not to come.

When Mr. Mojito joined me on the balcony, his face was dark with something. Anger? Concern? Hatred?

My body jittered with anxiety as I awaited his response. Did he know about his son and me? After the drama of Greta's attempted suicide, possibly her announcement that she was pregnant with his baby, had Mojito spilled his guts to his dad?

I suckled my injured tongue, trying to look normal, while my agitated fiancé loomed above me. Our eyes met, locked. With a sudden lunge, he grabbed my shoulders, his face inches from mine. I was grateful I smelled of coffee instead of booze. He kissed me on the forehead, then hugged me tightly. My face was pressed against the bottom of his silky Armani suit jacket.

"Thank God I have you to talk to," he murmured.

Relieved, I wrapped my arms around him and hugged him back. He smelled outdoorsy, like fresh pine needles. Idly, I wondered what that could be from. Didn't he spend all his time in office buildings? I knew so little about his work. What he did all day, what he did on his many business trips.

"Let me get you a drink. Or coffee?" I asked.

He sighed and pushed himself away gently. "Stay here with me. I need to talk to you."

I did as he said. He sat down on the deck chair beside me, then put his head in his hands. His hair ran though his tanned fingers. I reached over, stroking the back of his neck gently. "Tell me. Is it Mojito?"

My voice was steady. Since I already knew the soap opera plot of that teen drama, I could handle the "news" with a combination of warm empathy and cool detachment. An appropriate response from the future stepmom.

He sighed deeply, then sat up straight and cleared his throat. His face was wet. My heart went out to him. Poor, poor Mr. Mojito.

"My son's always been trustworthy. Smart, never a risk taker. And mature for his age. No trouble. Ever. But now?" He looked down at his feet and shook his head. Dejected, a beaten man. "Now he's made some bad choices. And he's in trouble."

"Is it the girlfriend?" I asked in a low voice. Secretly elated that *I* wasn't the one in trouble. Because I so easily could have been. After all, Mr. Mojito had caught us together. Once, only once. But still, that might have been enough to ruin everything.

It had happened at the Mojitos' place. My fiancé had disappeared inside to fetch coffee, and I was relaxing in the morning sun, waiting for him. It was a pleasant day and I was stretched out on a rattan couch on the cusp of the great lawn, admiring the view of the placid Intracoastal and inhaling the wild scent of the flowers in the garden. In South Florida, everything blooms year round. That day I remember the hibiscus blossoms were as big as my fist, fat balls of soft peach, hot pink, and blood red. There were rosebuds too. And pale pink frangipani. Gorgeous.

Speaking of gorgeous, suddenly Mojito wandered up. He was dressed in tight slacks and a baby-blue T-shirt, and he was munching an apple. He grinned between bites, then sat down beside me. When I moved over, he scooted closer.

"Don't," I said.

He lay down, resting his head in my lap, still crunching his apple. "Mommy," he said in this little boy's voice. "If I swallow an apple seed will an apple tree grow in my belly?"

Cute.

I spoke in a singsong voice too. "Yes, and your penis will grow big as a tree branch."

"Oh, Mommy, you'll love that, won't you?"

We were laughing when Mr. Mojito walked up behind us, a pot of coffee in one hand, the newspaper tucked under his arm.

Startled, we stared up at him, silent, unmoving. Caught, a couple of stupid deer in the headlights.

Mr. Mojito smiled. He looked down at us together like that and he smiled warmly. He said, "One big happy family, eh?" He seemed genuinely pleased.

Mojito stood and, without looking at me, sauntered away. He'd left his apple core on the cushion beside me. I picked it up, placed it on the glass coffee table, patted the seat beside me.

My fiancé took his rightful seat and we resumed our normal

Sunday routine. The *Times*, coffee, afternoon lovemaking. I always left for my place by dinnertime.

My fiancé was so distraught, I was not sure what I could do. I knelt down before him on the concrete floor of my patio and took his face in my hands, guiding his eyes to mine. "Tell me," I said. He was my friend. I would help him with his trouble, whatever it was.

He saw that there, in my eyes. "Oh, Cath. Our boy's gotten involved with the wrong girl." I loved how he said that. *Our boy.* "She's the daughter of a man we do not want to mess with. A *family* we do not want to mess with."

I looked at him blankly until the last word he'd emphasized clicked in my mind. "You mean a *family* family? Like, a *Sopranos*-type family?"

My fiancé nodded once, his expression grim. "Yes, exactly that. Apparently, the father had quite the business going in New Jersey. Still does, although they live here now. Mojito tells me he went out with her casually, tried to break it off. The girl did not respond well to his wishes. She was angry, acted out. And now she claims she's pregnant."

So, the gossipers at school had the right dirt after all. Silently, I thanked them for leaking it to me. A girl should always be prepared in any crisis. In order to remain appropriately chill and in control.

"Who told you all this?" I asked, standing up, placing both hands on my lover's head. The wisps of silver gray in his hair were lovely, but a constant reminder of my husband-to-be's advancing age. "I mean, are you sure?"

He wrapped his arms around my hips, snuggled his face against me and held on tight. Muffled against my crotch, his voice sounded far away when he said, "Mojito. He doesn't know what to do. He's scared out of his mind."

I bet. Jesus, what a mistake. She was nothing, cheap thrills, definitely not worth his time. Unless he'd gone out with her just to make me jealous? In which case, no matter how flattering it might feel, the whole mess was my fault.

"Shit," I said.

Mr. Mojito laughed. A sad, frightened sound. I never swore around him. He was such a gentleman.

"Sorry," I added.

But then he kissed my crotch through the fabric of my skirt. And the next thing I knew, he was removing my clothing and kissing me all over.

Men. They make love when they do not know what else to do. Or say.

Naked and chilled, I managed to pull him inside the condo. I tried to manipulate him into accompanying me to the bedroom, but he didn't want to walk that far. It was like he was starving for me, wild and desperate for my body, my love. The man had to have me right then, right there.

Who was I to say no?

We slid to our knees, then to the floor. Thank God for the throw rug or my back would have been seriously bruised. As it was, I ended up with a nasty rug burn on my tailbone and a terrible snarl in my hair that took an hour to comb out.

After he was done, he lay beside me on the living room floor. He said, "Cathriona, you saved me tonight. I still don't know what to do for my son, but now I know I have the strength to do what must be done."

Propped on one elbow, I leaned over to kiss his handsome face, his slightly sagging neck, his softly rounder shoulder. Such a good man. He tried so hard for those he loved. What I thought but didn't say was this: he would never do what needed to be done to help Mojito. He wasn't the kind of man who could do such a thing. Not Mr. Mojito. He cared too much, he was a moral person. So he couldn't reach out the slow clean hand of crime.

But I could.

That was what I thought about after that. How *I* could do just that.

17

In class the next afternoon, Mojito slumped in his seat. His hair flopped around his ears, uncombed, his eyes downcast. He looked like he hadn't slept in days. We carefully avoided each other's eyes while I lectured on the lack of narrative arc in post-postmodern literature. After class, I stood by my desk, phone in hand.

As expected, he texted me from the back row, where he sat waiting for the rest of the class to dribble out the door.

Fuck me. Now what?

I hid my smile. He was mine now. You see, he had nobody else to turn to. Nowhere else to go.

I put my phone in my handbag, strode from the classroom.

He didn't follow me. He would wait, try again. My Mojito was not stupid, but he could be quite aggressive, doggedly persistent, as demanding as his father. More so, on occasion.

Every woman loves a fascist. I loved two of them.

One night weeks earlier, I was home alone. It was cold, a strange chill wind descending on us from the Canadian tundra. The palm trees bent to the ground, lawn chairs tossed about on the condo pool deck. As darkness set in, the temperature dropped from sixty to forty and was expected to dip even lower overnight. *Brrrr.*

I had removed a down comforter from the hope chest at the foot of my bed, and I was airing it out on the balcony. Once I finished writing, I planned on taking a long hot bath and cuddling up in bed with my furry kitties for a nice wintry nap. We don't get to do this much down here in the tropics. I actually enjoyed the brisk change of pace.

I was two glasses into a blood-warming bottle of Cab Mr. Mojito had left behind the prior evening when there was a loud knock on the door. I wasn't expecting anyone. My fiancé was out of town until the weekend and, as you may have gathered this far into my story, I was virtually friendless. Which is how I like it. People are a bother. They suck up your energy like vampires, give you nothing but their petty problems in return for your wasted time with them.

Both cats scattered to their hiding spots. They were even more introverted than I was. Setting my laptop on the coffee table, I tiptoed to the front door and looked through the peep-hole. Instantly, the blood coursed through my body, heating me up from head to sole. I flung open the door and grabbed his arm, pulling him inside.

"Are you out of your mind? What if somebody sees you? I told you not to come here."

He stood in the entryway, shivering. No coat, just a tight T-shirt. He stared down at me, his face somber. Did I look like an old hag? Reading glasses on, no makeup, and I was dressed in baggy jeans and a denim shirt, my warmest clothes. My hair was all over the place. I tend to fiddle with it when I'm writing.

Suddenly his face shifted and he snickered. "I'm scared, Mommy. I can't sleep. It's too windy tonight." He moved to the side and pushed forward, as if to pass me on his way into the living area.

I wasn't amused. "Listen, baby," I said, blocking his entrance to my home. "I'm busy. And you shouldn't be here. It's not proper."

His nasty grin widened and he hooted. "Proper? *Proper?* You seduce me, you ball me blind, then you act like we have some formal agenda we're following? You're too fucking much, lady."

True.

He wasn't in on my plan for our future, however. He had no idea that much of my behavior was intentional. He was acting purely on his own primitive desires. He'd already overstepped, and now he wanted more.

Then again, I was the predator, the sexual monster in the eyes of a hypocritical and moralistic world. I was the adult, the person responsible for this parody of incest. Had I gone to a competent shrink, there might have been no disaster. But I chose instead to follow my own throbbing heart. So how could I say no when my love said yes, yes, yes?

I drew back against the wall, giving in to him, to his urges. Mojito barged past me into the living room. I smelled alcohol. He'd been drinking again, working up his courage. This made me sick with self-recognition.

He was looking around the messy room for clues about me. He would find none. What he was seeking lay deep in a file in my laptop. But he would never see what I had written about him. About his father. About my innermost thoughts and ideas and feelings. He would never know me. Not like that.

Still, the boy did his best.

"Can I offer you a cup of strong coffee?" I asked pointedly as I walked into the kitchen. Before I reached the coffeemaker, however, he tackled me from behind. "Don't," I said, but his hands were already on my breasts, and I was already dampening.

He held my breasts carefully, like a couple of softballs in his hands. I didn't move but my breathing sped up. His fingers slid easily under my shirt, cold on my bare skin. He played with my nipples, raising them to pebbled nubs. I let out a soft moan, an involuntary sound.

He laughed. "I won't do anything you don't want me to do, Dr. O."

His hands, warmed from my flesh, slid down my then flatter-belly and into my baggy jeans. Oh God, oh God. Mojito.

He nibbled the side of my neck, suckling his way up to my ear and inside it. His tongue was sharp, but he softened it, darting it in and out until my knees weakened. His hands moved to a rhythm and I felt it building inside my blood, my nerves, all my pulsating cells.

A good student, Mojito had learned on our very first night exactly what I needed from him. And he was willing to give that to me. He stopped for a moment, waiting for me to beg.

He liked that part.

"Please?" I said softly. Then I leaned into him, arching my hips into his capable hands. The rhythm continued and the waves swept over me. I closed my eyes and all I saw was Mojito. The boy, the young man, the lover I had always dreamed of.

And so he had me. Or, should I say, we had one another. On the kitchen floor. In the hot bath I had planned on taking alone. In the warm bed under the bulky comforter. And again in the darkness of the early morning.

I was not cold on that long chilly night. In fact, I burned.

Burn, Cathriona, burn.

Before it was light, I ushered him out. He had bedhead, his eyes ringed and tired looking. But he was smiling when he said, "See you at school, Dr. O."

He leaned in but I refused to kiss him. "Go," I hissed.

He looked crestfallen. I pushed his shoulder, pointed to the elevator. The hallway was empty, it was still early. He needed to leave without attracting attention. If we were seen, I might not be able to marry his father. It would be dangerous to continue with my plan for the future. For Mojito and me. But if nobody saw him, my plan could remain intact.

How would I even know if anyone in the building saw my young lover that cold morning, you ask? How would I know if someone noticed the boy, dazed with lust, reeking of sex, stumbling down to the parking lot? I wouldn't know, of course. Not until it was too late.

From the balcony, I watched him lope across the guest lot to his car. The red BMW, the one his dad bought him when Mojito turned sixteen. Only a year earlier.

He clutched his arms to his chest, his untucked shirt flapping in the wind. The morning air was still chilly. My love looked so small. Vulnerable. And so young.

As I was walking down the hall to the teacher's lounge, another text arrived from my bewildered boy. *That's it? You're not going to help me out?*

I stopped to text back. *Not now. Tonight.*

Then I put my phone away and went about my day.

When he texted me at midnight from down in the guest lot, I was ready for him. I waited a minute, then texted him back. He came right up. I had become brave over time, taking more chances and allowing him to visit me when it was impossible for us to have one another at his house. Or outside somewhere. On the beach. In an empty park. In the backseat of my cramped Volvo.

This time I had prepared for his visit. Makeup on. Hair washed. Shaved and perfumed and delightfully half dressed in silky short-shorts and a loose top. No bra, no panties. On my way to the door, I mussed my hair a little for that just-awakened look. I wanted him to think I'd been asleep, his predicament forgotten.

As soon as I opened the door, he pushed inside and past me. As always, I checked the hall for nosy neighbors. None in sight. I locked the door and followed my boy into the kitchen, where I leaned against the counter and forced a lazy yawn.

"So?" I said, pretending to rub my eyes.

He had a bottle of my tequila in hand and was searching the cabinets for a glass. I pushed him aside, lifted two tumblers from a shelf over the sink.

He smelled of fear. And lust. But not alcohol. He was trembling so much the booze sloshed in the bottle.

When I saw this, I stopped my phony distant act. "Honey, you're shaking." I took the bottle from him. "Go sit on the couch. You need something to eat too?"

He shook his head. His eyes were wide and bright, darting about, frightened. He looked like a scared kid.

He *was* a scared kid.

I followed him into the living room with the bottle and glasses. I waited until he dropped onto the couch, then poured him a big glass. He drank it right down, held out his glass for more.

I sat down next to him on the couch, poured him a smaller glass. Down it went. He shivered, closed his eyes. He held out the glass again.

I gave him mine.

Finally, he spoke. "She says it's mine but I doubt that. I think it's a game she's playing. To what end, I have no idea. Money?"

I wasn't following but could put two and two together to get the sum total of a paranoid kid shirking responsibility.

Not that I blamed him.

"Maybe she loves you. Is she Catholic?" I asked. Weren't all those mobsters from churchgoing families? Or was that just on TV? "I mean, what about an abortion?"

He didn't open his eyes, just shook his head. "She's out of her mind. *Let's get married, have a family! I know, you can work for my dad!*" He looked at me when he imitated her squeaky voice, the Jersey accent. His eyes were full of something I'd never seen before. An undertow of illness. It sucked at me, but I resisted.

"Is she seeing anyone else? Sleeping around?" I poured more tequila, a little worried. This dumb chick might ruin all my plans. She could singlehandedly destroy my future with Mojito. "I mean, could it—?"

"I slept with her the first time after Dad told me you guys were engaged. And then you and I... Oh God, I didn't know what to do. I was confused."

He wouldn't look at me. Still, my heart pulsed with his. He loved me. Not her.

I reached for his hand, but he pulled away. "She said she was a virgin. But it didn't seem that way to me. And after, she told me she loved me. I didn't say anything back. I felt bad then. I feel bad now. I feel bad all the fucking time!"

This spilled out in a burst of sudden anger.

He shot up from the couch, paced the floor. "But I don't feel anything for *her*. I hang with her a lot at school, give her next to nothing. Then go out with her on the weekends. To parties, to the beach. But only to fuck with *your* head." He frowned, paced, refused to catch my eye. "I used protection, for fuck's sake. How could she have—?"

"Don't be a fool. Condoms fail. She's young, fertile. Did you sleep through sex ed?"

My tone must have been too sharp because he headed for the front door. I had to chase him down, grab his arm and pull him back to the living room. "Sorry. I'm sorry, baby. You've got to calm down. Look, why are you here? What do you want from me?" I asked, my hand still gripping his rigid arm. "I mean, are you looking for advice? Sex? Comfort? Tell me what you want from me."

Finally, he spilled. His monologue was long and disorganized. But the gist of it was this: Greta was unstable, she had a childhood history of acting out, shrink visits, weak suicide attempts. A lot of that had to do with her overbearing father. Of course, the old man adored her. He also controlled her. Told her he wanted her to find the right guy and settle down some day. He'd convinced her a career was unimportant, that finding a good partner and having a family was what would stabilize her. She was under her dad's spell and so she was all about that too, believing marriage was the answer to her issues. When Mojito came along, confused and horny, apparently she'd seen him as the key to her future. The future her dad wanted for her. Now she claimed she was pregnant, the baby was his, and, if he didn't marry her, she'd kill herself.

He said, "I doubt she'd do that. I'm not sure she's even pregnant. The girl is crazy. But if she tells her dad, he will hurt me. Seriously hurt me. My dad says he'll talk to Mr. Cantoli. But I don't think that'll work. I'm royally fucked, Cath."

Mojito looked into my eyes. His love was all mixed up. With confusion, fear, self-pity, rage. The undertow sucked at me hard, harder. I felt the massive pull, the unleashing turmoil, the thrash of a fierce and deadly sea.

My turn to feel afraid. I let go of his arm.

"I want you to help me get Greta off my back," he said. "I think you owe me that."

He was right. Plus, I'd been thinking the same thing. Only

my thoughts were far darker than his. I was considering permanent solutions to his problem. To *our* problem.

When I reached for the bottle of tequila, it was practically empty. Mojito collapsed on the couch while I went to the kitchen to hunt down more booze.

18

Afew weeks later, Mr. Mojito bought a boat. A teal and teak motor yacht I talked him into purchasing. Why live on the water if you aren't going to enjoy it?

At least this was what I'd said to my aging lover. I repeated this several times, then brought up the subject again one evening just after we'd made love.

He rolled over on his side to look at me. His eyes were filled with something rich. Gratitude? Satisfaction? I'm not sure, but it was real, and it was pure. If I'd been the kind of person who felt guilt, I might have turned away in shame. Instead, I smiled at him. Sweetly.

He brushed a stray hair from my face. "I didn't think you were a water person, Cath."

True. In fact, I hated the water. I rarely went in his pool, preferring to lounge beside it. Jumped in and out of the shallow end on occasion, like when I had to for the sake of appearance. Because of a childhood incident, drowning was one of my biggest fears. I doubted I could even swim. Imagine that, living in Florida, smack on the beach, and not being confident I could stay afloat.

But with my fiancé, I made a cutesy face. "But I love it when you talk about your old boats. You enjoyed them. I want to learn to sail with you. Fish. We can go to the islands. Snorkel. Dive. Watch the dolphins and the manatees."

Of course, I had no interest in doing any of that. But my fiancé loved the water. And the idea of sharing adventures with me made him happy.

He kissed me on the lips, then worked his way down. The deal was done.

After that, he shopped boats online. He'd had three or four of them in the past so he knew what he was looking for. When he found a secondhand motor yacht he liked docked at a marina in Fort Lauderdale, he made the call.

I drove down with him to look it over. He told me the boat was named *Clytemnestra*. In Greek mythology, she was quite the troublemaker. An adulteress, a murderer. This didn't seem to bother my husband-to-be.

The day was bright and clear, cloudless, the water calm. The seller greeted us on the dock. A weather-beaten man in a striped jersey and a jaunty cap, he chatted with Mr. Mojito, then invited us aboard. The boat was pretty, not too big, not too fancy. Still, I was nervous just stepping onto the glossy wood deck.

When the Intracoastal water rocked gently beneath my feet, I felt queasy. I stood in the middle of the fore deck, afraid to look over the side. I imagined enduring hours of the same motion with nothing beneath me except fathoms of cold, cold water.

Gulp.

To take my mind off my unsettled stomach, I wandered around. The men were up above in the pilot's area, looking at the computers and talking numbers. The boat was old but impressive, all shine and gleam. It had a little cabin down below with a queen-size bed and a white-tiled bathroom. Dual shower heads. Not bad for something that could kill me just by leaning to the side.

I went upstairs to join my fiancé. He cocked his head, lifting one graying eyebrow. *You like?* he asked silently.

I nodded, smiling. *Buy it*, my expression urged.

The seller claimed he'd been all over the Atlantic in that little boat. Just the idea of it gave me claustrophobia. I turned away, looked down into the pale-green depths. The water was like a polished Coke bottle. Big gray shadows drifted up and under the boat.

"Tarpon," the seller said. "Beautiful, aren't they?"

I nodded, mesmerized. And sick to my stomach. I re-swallowed this morning's eggs, somehow keeping the ridiculous plastic smile on my face.

Mr. Mojito wrote him a check right there.

A few days later, Mojito helped his dad collect their new boat, motoring up the Intracoastal Waterway. By the time they arrived at the house, the boy seemed to know what he was doing. I watched from the rattan couch on the back lawn as my young man docked the boat. His dad jumped out, securing it with two ropes.

I quick dunked in the pool, then wandered down to the dock wet, shaking the water from my hair. I wanted to look seaworthy. My fiancé was on deck, beer bottle in hand. He waved me aboard. Mojito came up from below with two more bottles of Heineken, his face alight with sun and happiness. They both seemed jubilant.

Boys and their toys.

I joined them on the deck and Mojito handed me a cold one. Our fingers brushed, the electricity sparking deep in my loins. We avoided one another's eyes.

We sat down with his dad and they launched into a discussion of their plans for the boat. Head up to Peanut Island on Saturday, for cocktail hour and a fish grill. Maybe the trop rock concert at the vineyard in Port St. Lucie the following weekend. Cruise to Virginia Key, Key West, the Ten Thousand Islands wildlife refuge.

The three of us.

Oh yeah, I was a water girl. At least, that was the impression I gave.

After an hour or so, I left for home to get dressed for our dinner out. Closely following my instructions, Mojito had invited Greta to join us. I was to give her a talking to, see if I could change her attitude. And, if that didn't work, I had more ominous plans. The *Clytemnestra* could make my job easier. If I worked up my courage.

A big *if*.

All dolled up in the Ralph Lauren he'd recently bought for me, I met my fiancé at the Boca Club at six. The young folks were late, so my date and I were deep into a lively bottle of Beaujolais by the time they arrived at the candlelit patio bar. Mr. Mojito had not been introduced to his son's girlfriend, and I had not had her as a student. We knew who she was though. What she was. So we had warned one another to be nice. Very nice.

And there she was. Bone thin and child faced. Ever the gentleman, at least in public, Mojito introduced us.

I stuck out a hand to greet her. I was pleased to see how unattractive she was close up. Maybe it was the lighting, but she looked like a waif. Anorexic, anemic. Push her over with a duck feather. Her skinny little paw felt like an ice cube in my hand.

Her overbite needed fixing, but her perky tits had already been perfected. Parents who pay for cosmetic surgery on their teenage daughters should be arrested for child abuse.

And this girl was indeed a child. Her red velveteen miniskirt barely covered her narrow thighs, and her tiny feet were tucked into shiny black flats. All she needed was a pair of white bobby sox and a giant lollipop and her Betty Boop costume would be complete.

Still, I said, "So happy you could join us tonight, Greta. Now don't tell the other kids at school, okay?"

She nodded, all smiles and giggles. Of course, she would post tonight's dinner party details on Facebook before the evening was over. And talk about nothing else for a week. The Boca Club was *the* place to see and be seen. Especially if you were a cheesy Jersey chick.

Mojito pulled out a chair and my competition sat down with an awkward plop. She failed to thank him, staring around the outdoor dining area with wide heavily made-up eyes. Looking for the city's top players, no doubt. So she could tweet about it later. *Leo was there with a really hot supermodel. And Suze Orman ate a jellied salad with her girlfriend!*

I sipped my wine and kept my glass in hand so Mr. Mojito wouldn't fill it again. I needed to be in control so I could steer the girl where I wanted to go.

The girl looked at Mojito and smiled. She had a lovely smile. Jealousy surged through my bloodstream. I would be sure to buttress my patience lest I say something mean and blow my cover. And what was my cover? The aloof lit professor with a secret life among the one percent, the *über*-rich, currently dating a distinguished sixty-year-old millionaire.

That was me, all right.

Mojito seated himself next to me. Under the table, he rested a hand on my knee and squeezed.

Instantly, I relaxed. He was mine, all mine.

I leaned forward to speak to Greta, who was texting someone on the phone she'd set down on the linen tablecloth. "No phones at the dinner table, hon."

With a start, she stopped what she was doing and slipped it in her Gucci bag. "Oops." She even blushed a little.

Game on.

"So," my fiancé said. "What are your college plans, Greta?" He smiled at his son's date, but his cool expression masked his deep concern.

"C'mon, Dad," Mojito intervened. "Get the girl a drink before you grill her."

"Pour the kids some wine," I instructed. "Unless you think management will object?"

Greta slid her glass forward.

Hmm. Really? Would a pregnant kid drink alcohol? Unlike my generation and the women who preceded us, today's kids were heavily indoctrinated. Fetal alcohol syndrome. Genetic damage. Physical and mental abnormalities.

But she'd also had sex ed classes since age eight. Maybe Greta was a poor student.

She gulped her wine. Mojito let his glass sit. Under the table, he stroked my thigh. The inside of my thigh. High up.

This was the most fun I'd had in weeks.

"I don't want to go to college," Greta blurted. She followed up with a shrug of her narrow shoulders. "I want to have a family. Like my mom."

Mr. Mojito gave me the look. *What the hell?*

I said to her, "You're young. You've got plenty of time for that. So, what's your favorite subject in school? You don't have to say English just because I'm here."

Everyone laughed. Mojito gave me a grateful stroke. I had to push his hand away or I'd never make it through the meal.

Greta got peppy. She thrived on being the center of attention. "I'm good at math. Computer science. I have that kind of brain. If I didn't already have plans for my future, I might've wanted to be a software engineer. I like physics too."

Who knew?

"Why not do that first, then have a family?" I asked. "I delayed marriage for my career and have zero regrets."

She looked me up and down, her mind racing. I could imagine what she was thinking. Too bad and now you're an old bag, or something along those lines.

"Which is my good fortune," my dear fiancé said. Then he reached across the table to hold my hand. So sweet.

Greta melted. Her eyes teared up, and she blotted them with a pink napkin. Wow, was the girl hormonal? Or just sappy? When I poured the rest of the wine into her glass, she smiled at me gratefully.

Game over.

A tuxedoed waiter appeared with menus and Mr. Mojito ordered another bottle of red, a costly Bordeaux. The conversation turned to Peanut Island and both kids told us about the partying that went on every weekend. They'd been a few times with friends. But not with each other.

"If we go, will Mr. Mojito and I be the only adults on the island?" I asked, smiling at my fiancé.

The kids exchanged glances.

"No. But after dark, it changes from families and fishing to heavy drinking. Drugs. Loud music." Mojito looked at his dad. "Let's just go for the afternoon."

His father agreed. Then we ordered our meals and chatted about world events. The upcoming election. The situation in the Middle East. Immigration and terrorism and the drug cartels. Opioid addiction. The overloaded prison system.

To my surprise, the girl spoke intelligently and held her

tongue when she had nothing to say. I almost liked her. She had potential. Why try to ensnare a pretty rich boy? What was the point of that?

Fear, I guess. And programming. Or direct instructions. The thought of meeting her father sent chills up and down my spine. I sipped a little wine until my body warmed again.

When the appetizers arrived, Greta excused herself to go to the ladies room. Terrible timing, but why not? So I said, "I'll join you."

It was time for that girl talk I'd promised Mojito.

Greta and I walked inside the clubhouse and I led the way down the sconce-lit hallway to the restrooms. "You ever been here before?" I asked her.

Of course she hadn't. "My parents only take us to Italian restaurants." Her grin was sharp. "I can tell you the best pizza places from here to Miami."

We laughed, then I held the door for her. We were alone in the black and white bathroom. All the stall doors were painted a god-awful blood red.

"I feel like I'm in a Tim Burton movie," she said with a snort.

I *did* like her.

Shit.

"So, how long have you lived in the area?" I called out from my stall. "You're from New Jersey, right?"

"Yeah. We used to come down on vacations before my dad retired. Then he said we had to move here. I was in ninth grade. Believe me, I did *not* want to leave the Shore. But now I love it here."

I flushed, waited for her at the porcelain sinks. "So you don't want to go back north? After you graduate, I mean."

She washed her hands thoroughly. Soaping them, even. Raised right, this girl.

"Nope. I love the water. I love the weather. And I love Mojito."

We caught eyes in the gilded mirror over the sinks. "I know you understand. I can see you love him too."

I must have looked startled because she laughed. "Mr. Mojito, I mean."

Flashing a fake grin, I said, "I do. They're both great guys. Gentlemen. You don't meet many of those anymore. Not good-looking rich ones anyway."

I took out a hairbrush and primped while she reapplied her lipstick. Too red. It made her look like Snow White.

"So are you two like serious?" she asked me. Bold now. Like we were girlfriends at a school dance. "I mean, you do want to marry him, right?"

I shrugged. "Why would I do that? I have my own life. I have a good job. Why give that up?"

I kept brushing my hair. It was going to fall out if I didn't stop, but I wanted to see how far she would go with me.

Her eyes widened. "Are you kidding? Why work when you can travel the world, live in a mansion, and dine at the best restaurants every night?" She was so young. So naïve. Poor girl. "I mean, don't you want to have children? Or is it too late for that?"

Ouch. How old did she think I was? "No, I don't want kids. I made that decision years ago. And I can have the lifestyle without becoming some man's wife. Keep my independence *and* enjoy myself." Had nobody spoken frankly to this generation about a woman's freedom and the right to choose? "Why are you so anxious to give all that up? You have decades of fun and excitement ahead of you. Years of doing what you want before you have to even *think* about becoming a wife and mother."

I dropped my hairbrush back in my purse, turned to face her. She seemed lost in thought. I launched into it. "When I was a teenager, I was crazy about this boy. Jacky. Captain of the football team. His father was a doctor. Jacky had everything going for him. Looks, money, brains, athletic ability. And major sex appeal."

This was off the cuff. Lifted from a story I wrote years before. Unpublished. Until now.

"I lost my virginity to that boy. Then I had a decision to make." I paused, allowing the tears to collect in my eyes. Ah, I should have been an actress. "I made the right one. I have no regrets."

I led the way out the door, then stopped in the dim hallway. She stood behind me, silent. She knew there was a punch line.

"Jacky became an alcoholic. He was arrested twice. For domestic violence."

She was silent all the way back to the table.

The oysters were delicious. So was the veal. I enjoyed the meal, and reveled in the reassuring press of Mojito's warm hand on my knee.

Greta ate little, and she seemed less bubbly. Distracted, maybe, and subdued. While the boys ordered dessert, I caught her looking at me across the table. When I smiled, she smiled in return. I thought I saw something in her pale face. Gratitude, perhaps.

Before we parted ways, she hugged me.

Shit. I really liked the kid.

19

S tanding at the arrival board, I'm bed tousled and anxiety ridden, looking at flight cancellations. Then I'm at the departure gate, running through the boarding tunnel, late for a connection. Or am I? Wait, should I be boarding? Wasn't I supposed to be meeting someone at the arrival gate? I stop, wondering. A moment later, water is everywhere. The ocean surrounds me. I float, then sink, then pop up gasping. What is this? How is this possible? Am I lost at sea? I see myself from above, treading water, alone in the vast wavering, the endless blue. A tiny fleck in a raging ocean, like Mark Wahlberg in his final scene in *The Perfect Storm*.

There it is, the perfect ending, I think. I deserve this, I deserve nothing. So go ahead, Life, submerge me, I think.

Then I go under.

The water is warm, and welcoming as a man's loving hand. Take me, is what I think as I drift down, down. I want only to be taken.

The room was quiet when I sat up, shaking myself awake. Alone in my bed in the early morning light, tucked under too much bedding. Hot nights make for wild dreams, at least this has always been true for me.

With a sigh, I eased out of bed, leaving behind the dead weight of the bedclothes. I was dry, on land, safe in my own head.

Or was I?

A few hours later, I was packing lunches for the trip to Peanut Island when my phone went.

Mojito.

I picked up. "Don't tell me you aren't coming today." The only reason I'd even get on that boat was to be with him. My Mojito. Even if I had to share him with Greta. "You better not back out now, bro."

"Always so quick to prejudge. No, I'll be aboard. But *she* won't." His voice was light, teasing. "Let's you and me leave the old man at home, have that rockin' stateroom all to ourselves. Christen it with a bottle of Dom."

Some day. Maybe even someday soon. But not yet.

I said, "Why isn't she coming? I thought she was all excited about today."

He paused. Maybe for dramatic effect. Then he laughed a little. "The sad fact is she broke up with me last night. Friended me, actually. Said she's going to get serious about her future. Like study for the SATs, go all out for the rest of her junior year. She's decided she wants to apply to MIT. Her aunt's like a dean or something there." He breathed deeply for a moment. "No mention of the fictional baby. So that devious subplot's been dropped from the script."

Maybe. Or maybe she thought about what I told her and set up an appointment to get it taken care of. On her own.

I said nothing. Manipulating the minds of the young was my specialty. Years of practice had perfected my skills. Case in point: Mojito still thought *he* was seducing *me*.

He took a different tack. "My father's in a celebratory mood. So bring your party hat, *cher*."

I smiled at the use of hip mardi gras lingo. "Will do, *cher*. And congrats on your newfound freedom. Don't be an ignoramus. Use it wisely."

Motherly advice, I know, but I meant it. I needed time to continue building the foundation for our life together. In the meantime, he needed to not get anyone else in a family way.

Was this too much to ask?

He grunted. Then the swift kick to the head. "I may meet Greta up there. See if she wants to hang. I mean as friends."

What happened to ditching his dad so we could cavort? I thought he might be fronting, so I said, "Of course. We'll have fun, the four of us."

Then I clicked off. And turned off my phone.

Later that morning I read his follow-up text. *Sorry. I know I'm an asshole sometimes. But I hate it when you act like you're my mom. I prefer us on even ground.*

That was a lie. He wanted me on my knees. His hands on my head. Like all men do.

I didn't hold it against him, it was natural. Primitive, instinctual, animal behavior. But, just to make him squirm, I ignored him on the boat. I hung around on the bridge with his father while we motored out of the Waterway to the clean green ocean. All the way north on that smooth glassy sea, I was all over his dad. I clung to him, my arms about his neck, whispering in his ear, nibbling it, kissing him passionately. A jolly good show.

Anything rather than look at the moving water. *Gulp.*

Anything rather than look into the sullen face of the boy I loved. Oh my lord, that beautiful face! Even pouting, he was just so adorable.

His father was in a joyful mood, drinking beer from the bottle, pointing out the various sea birds, joking with me about my greenish pallor. He kissed me back good-naturedly, basking in my enthusiastic bursts of affection.

As we approached our destination, the island waters grew increasingly crowded with anchored boats of all sizes. Big sailing yachts measuring more than two hundred feet from bow to stern, some with jet skis on the back, hot tubs on deck. Brightly colored cigarette boats, pastel catamarans. Canoes and kayaks and kids sitting or standing on sup boards. Tanned girls in g-string bikinis, blond boys in board shorts, Solo cups in tanned fists everywhere. The music from dozens of stereo systems blared pop rock. Country. Rap, a lot of rap. The air pulsed with sexual tension.

I caught my fiancé's eye as we circled the mass of boats anchored gunwale to gunwale. I raised one eyebrow and he frowned. It was still midday and already they were deep into an on-the-water rave. It was most definitely not our scene. In fact, I was afraid I'd run into some of my students and they would hold that against me. They might see it as spying, or at the very least trespassing on their turf.

"I'm way out of my element here," I said.

He agreed. "Maybe Mojito can locate his friends. Then you and I can head for Jupiter, have lunch at Jetty's."

Seafood? My stomach lurched.

"Sounds great," I said. I was seasick, and morning sick, and sick of being on the water. But what could I do? The boat had been my idea. "Do you have any crackers on board?"

He nodded, grinned. "Brought some especially for landlubbers. Down in the galley."

He meant in the windowless box that doubled as a kitchen. I stood, kissed the top of his head, and went down below to hunt for saltines. I settled on a bag of pretzel nuggets and stood there in the cool darkness, chewing on a dry salty tasteless mass. Ugh. I'd felt worse, but not without consuming gallons of booze beforehand.

Mojito appeared in the narrow doorway, filling it. The anger in his eyes elicited in me a heady mix of fear and desire. But I kept my face blank, crunching methodically.

"Pretzel?" I asked with a full mouth, holding out the bag.

"You kill me," he said. The waves rocked us, the sound of the splashing water like his palm against my face.

Not you, I thought. Never you.

"I feel like strangling you, tossing your lifeless body overboard." He didn't move toward me, so I kept eating. "Or else fucking you to death."

Ooh, talk to me like Tony Soprano, I thought with a wet little ping of excitement. The competition with the old man was bringing out the alpha dog hiding there inside my young man. I liked that.

He put his hands on his lean hips. His bathing trunks were tight enough that I could see he was excited. Bad boy. "Look, I'm outta here. Have lotsa fun with Dad. Maybe you two can play Frank Sinatra records and rub each other's calloused feet."

He waited for me to snarl back. Instead, I kept munching. Our eyes locked, held. I stopped jawing. He throbbed with raging heat and passion. His fury fueled my desire and I felt so far away I wanted to cry out. Run to him. Press him to me hard and harder, then take him inside me. And keep him there, where he belonged.

But I couldn't. Not yet.

With difficulty, I swallowed and licked crumbs off my dry lips. Then I shrugged. "Do what you want, kiddo. Just be sure to use protection. I'm not going to get you out of any more girl trouble."

His face reddened. His fists clenched, so tight I thought he might step forward and sock me. He didn't move though. Not for a tense and, for me, sexually exciting minute. I was sopping wet. Go ahead, touch me, I thought.

But he was too smart for that. He knew we wouldn't be able to stop ourselves if he did. So instead, he turned and fled.

I tried not to laugh. I really did. But it was just too ridiculous. The boy and his father. Two pregnant women. The party boats lined up, full of hormone-fueled teenagers. Me, seasick and morning sick and an emotional wreck. The spinster teacher, finally engaged to an available millionaire, yet madly, adolescently, stupidly in love with a kid. With possibly the most inappropriate person on the Atlantic seaboard.

I guffawed. In fact, I had a bit of a meltdown in the galley, trying to control my hysterics. Was it really that funny, or were my hormones as out of control as the kids'?

Once I stopped giggling, I felt sick again. Food wasn't helping. I put the pretzels away and trooped back up to the pilot's deck with the good news. The oldsters had been dismissed. Yay.

My fiancé was already up to date. "If you don't mind, I see no point in lingering. Mojito will make his own way back. Shall we find somewhere else to spend this beautiful afternoon? Somewhere more our style?"

"Good idea." I smiled my agreement. Hopefully, we'd soon be on dry land.

After he turned us around and headed south, Mr. Mojito pointed to a massive yacht. The thing was like a wedding cake, the multilayered decks cluttered with lean youth in skimpy bathing suits. "There's our boy," he said. "Where he should be. Having fun with the other kids."

Girls who aren't pregnant with his child, you mean, was what I thought. Then I took a closer look.

Teen girls in butt-nude bikinis. They dressed like the strippers did back in my day. Tanned buttocks were everywhere, and perky breasts in barely there tops. I had to admit, the chicks looked sizzling hot. What boy could resist? The girls were practically naked already.

Boys in flowered board shorts tossed a small football back and forth. Upstairs, a dreadlocked DJ spun vinyl. I could smell their suntan oil, the weed, keg beer. Kanye blasted across the water that separated us.

"No Church in the Wild." Oh yeah.

Then I spotted him. Mojito stood on the bottom deck. He was soaking wet from taking the water route over to his friends' boat. His broad back was to us, one arm draped around the narrow shoulders of the only person in the group lacking a tan.

She looked over her shoulder, waved.

Greta.

Mr. Mojito caught the action and his mood dampened. "I wish he wouldn't spend any more time with her. That girl's nothing but trouble."

"I don't know," I lied. "I like her. Besides, he'll get past her soon enough. He told me she's set her sights on getting into MIT. So maybe she'll focus on academics from now on instead of Mojito."

Unlikely, but one never knew with teenagers.

My lover saw through the false optimism. "You know as well as I do she's got her hooks in deep. We need to dissuade him from dating her. I don't want him involved with that family."

When Mr. Mojito put his arm around me, I could feel his muscles twitching. He was really upset. At the time, I didn't understand it. Later on, I did. Completely. But that day, all I thought about was how I needed to soothe his anxiety or our day would be ruined.

So I reassured him. "He already knows she's a drama queen. He's too smart to stay with that. He'll move on soon enough. Don't worry."

Mr. Mojito avoided my eyes when he replied. "You're a woman. You speak of practicalities. He's a man. Other drives govern his actions."

When I bent down to open the cooler at our feet, Mr. Mojito grabbed my ass. And held on. Possessively, I thought.

We motored south until we picked up the Jupiter River. Instead of stopping at Jetty's, however, we moored at Guanabanas, a tropical outdoor bar with lots of shade palms and thatched roofing to keep off the sun. I grabbed us a shady table and fanned myself with a plastic menu while my fiancé made himself useful at the bar. He came back with a couple of tall glasses filled with ice. And what looked like a murky iced tea.

That wouldn't work for me. "What have you done?" I joshed.

He smiled. His nose was pink from our hours in the sun, which made him appear youthful. Or more youthful. He still looked middle aged, alas.

"Long Island iced teas, baby. I haven't had one of these since —" He stopped suddenly, looked away. "Ever drink these, or were they popular way before your time?"

That, I liked. Him acknowledging my youth. Comparative youth, I should say. "I don't think I have. What's in it?"

"Almost everything," he said with a smile.

I took a sip. Powerful. Boozy. "This is going to go down way too fast."

"You look beautiful in this filtered light," he said, reaching for my chin and tilting my head slightly. "You could pass for one of those teenagers on Peanut Island."

Now he was stretching it. I managed a humble smile, flattered despite myself. "So are we eating or just drinking?"

"Whatever you want, baby."

He seemed content. Such a simple man. At home in his multimillion-dollar mansion, dining at the most exclusive club in snobby Boca Raton, standing at the helm of his boat, sitting on a rickety stool in a yachtie bar. Mr. Mojito could get along wherever he happened to be.

I looked around. The place was busy. Mostly red-faced older couples drinking long necks. A few families with burgers and onion rings, hyperactive towheads running loose. A couple of doggy mascots stretched out by their masters' barstools. Typical weekend boat crowd.

"You ever read Denis Johnson?" my fiancé suddenly asked. "*Jesus' Son?*"

Of course I had. But had he? Johnson was not well known, but he was greatly admired by other writers. I said, "I love Johnson's work. So stark. Compelling. Why do you ask?"

He shrugged. "I can see you writing stories like that. A bad protagonist making stupid mistakes on an isolated highway, in quiet neighborhoods, wherever he happens to be. But in your case, *she*. A troubled troublemaker, a dark but somehow sympathetic *she*."

I sat back. Had he somehow read my work? How could he have? None of it had been published.

Not yet, anyway.

I said, "I could never write like Denis Johnson, of course, but my work has some similarities. You might call it bad girl lit. But how did you know?"

My drink was all ice water. I sucked at it loudly through the plastic straw until he reached for the glass.

"I know *you*, Cathriona O'Hale," he said, standing up to head for the bar. To buy me another drink. He winked. "And I believe in you."

That brought a tiny tear to my eye. He was such a rare man. Well read. Erudite. Understanding of human nature. And so accepting of me. Why couldn't I want him, instead of his underage son?

I watched my fiancé saunter up to the bar, lean in to place the order. His hair was thinning on the back of his head. In the harsh sun's glare, I could see the patch of scalp that shone there. Like a beacon to advancing age.

I turned away to stare at the quiet blue water. Too, too bad.

Later, when we were moored again at the dock outside the house, he made love to me in the stateroom. This was our first time in that small and windowless room. Between the rocking of the boat, the one-and-a-half Long Island teas I'd had for lunch, and my crazed hormones, I couldn't catch my breath. This seemed to please him.

When he released, his apelike yodel could have been heard by the kids still partying on Peanut Island.

20

After that, I blocked Mojito's calls and made it a point to ignore him in school. Of course, I watched him secretly. Especially when he was with Greta.

I enjoyed the game at first, but he played it a little too well. Whenever I saw him, he seemed to nuzzle up to her or text someone (her, most likely). He was never around the house anymore when I was there. Did not join us for dinner or sunset cruises on *Clytemnestra*. And his term paper was noticeably late.

I thought about setting up a parent-teacher conference with Mr. Mojito, but this seemed ludicrous. Besides, we were busy with our wedding plans and I didn't want to spoil his mood. He was in charge of everything. The ceremony. The party at the house. The honeymoon, which he'd decided would consist of Caribbean island hopping in the new boat. Whatever, I was apathetic about the whole thing. Let him have his fun, I simply agreed to everything he said he wanted.

My reward would come soon enough.

In the meantime, I was more than two months along and the bump had sweetened to a small bulge. I grew increasingly worried about being discovered. Pretty soon I would need to tell my fiancé the "good news."

One scorching Sunday afternoon, I drove to Total Wine and purchased a bottle of alcohol-free champagne. (Brut, actually. No French château would sell champagne sans alcohol.) No alcohol? What was the point? Well, if I walked into the Mojitos' house flashing that silly excuse for a celebratory drink, the game would be on. My man was bright enough. He'd know what no booze for me signified for us.

I wasn't worried about his reaction. I was predicting pure unadulterated joy on his end. What old guy with an almost grown kid doesn't want to be told he's still got what it takes? How virile a man feels when his woman says the magic words, *I'm carrying your child.*

Not that I could say this with any confidence. Was the baby his? Or his son's? But still. My aging fiancé was sure to be thrilled.

At this point, you are probably wondering about my own attitude toward baby on board. Was I still drinking? Yes, but less. Was it too late to have things taken care of? No, it was not. Did I want to be a mother? Absolutely not. But did I have at hand the very best insurance policy available for any woman about to marry an attractive millionaire? You bet.

The day was hot and sultry so I drove with the windows up, air down low. When I pulled up in front of the house, the Rolls was there. So was Mojito's BMW. And snugged up behind it, a black van with heavily tinted windows.

Cops or kidnappers?

Then I noticed the New Jersey plates. Greta's people?

I left the bottle on the passenger seat and walked around the side of the house through the thick brush. I wasn't planning on spying. Not really. That was not the original intention. But once I heard all the yelling, remaining hidden turned out to be the best move. So that's exactly what I chose to do.

Their voices were distinct, the discussion heated. Two men in a verbal battle, Mr. Mojito and somebody with a Jersey snarl. I squatted down at the corner of the house, then peeked around to check out who was in the backyard with my fiancé. A massive black guy in a tight suit blocked my view. He had to be six-five. Shiny bald head. Gun lump behind his left shoulder. Wow. Thick arms crossed, long legs spread wide, he had the stance of a soldier at the gate. Bodyguard, I guessed. He sure looked the part.

"You knew who you were dealing with from the get-go, pal." Jersey guy's voice sounded angry, threatening. "He wants out now, he gets out now. That's how it works wit' him. So don't think you can avoid responsibility with your finance and banking regs bullshit."

I wasn't watching anymore, just leaning against the side of the house, listening. The water bounced the sound back, but still, I couldn't catch everything they said. The argument had something to do with a client's investments, that much was clear. And nothing to do with the maternity issues of Greta Cantoli. I reminded myself that New Jersey was a populous state and lots of the residents enjoyed spending part of the year in the South Florida area. The visitors were probably not related to Mojito's squeeze.

"You don't come here unannounced and tell me what to do with my private fund!" My fiancé's voice grew louder until he was shouting. I'd seen him upset, weepy, worried, but never angry. I'd never even heard him raise his voice before. I like it when a man shows his balls. And it took balls to yell at a guy who traveled with protection straight out of central casting. "So take your fucking monkey and get off my property."

I snickered. Mr. Mojito being politically incorrect? This was another side he'd never showed me. My nipples hardened. My lover had more grit than I'd imagined.

But my smile evaporated after he added, "And tell your boss he'll get his money. But not this way. Not like this."

What? Mr. Mojito was a millionaire who ran a private equity firm to invest for himself and a few other super wealthy investors. So why would he owe anybody...?

I heard the thud of their approaching footsteps. Meeting over, apparently.

I turned and fled down the cedar chip pathway, zipping around the house, then jogging across the driveway. At my car, I posed, leaning in the passenger window as if to fetch the bottle. I remained in that position, bottom up for show, even after I heard their footsteps scuffle onto the gravel drive.

"He's fuckin' with us," the one who had been talking to Mr. Mojito said, heavy on the Jersey accent.

"Look at this place, though," the other guy said. He had no accent. "He's good for it."

"Fuck you talking about? Man's probably squatting. Or living here on ever'body else's investments. Another fuckin' Bernie."

Bernie? Bernie who? Sanders?

One of them whistled. My signal to end the pose.

I stood and straightened my skirt, then tucked the bottle under my arm. The black guy didn't look at me. The other one stopped whistling and gave me a bold stare. Short, fat, pock-marked. He tipped an imaginary hat, said, "Ma'am."

They climbed into the van. The black guy started up the engine.

When the passenger window eased down, I was close by, at the bottom of the short staircase leading to the front door. I turned around to look at them, hip cocked suggestively.

"You're a fine-looking lass," the fat guy said.

I stared in his round brown eyes. He looked a bit simian. His ears stuck out, his bite was long. He twisted his thin lips into an apelike smile. Maybe *he* was the monkey.

"What's a beautiful babe like you doin' wit' a scumbag like him?" he asked, his tone oddly confidential.

Those Italian men, they like me. I'd experienced that kind of attention from them all my life. I wasn't sure why they went for me, but normally I flirted back. Now I wasn't sure what to say or do. Defend Mr. Mojito? Run up the stairs? Act flattered? Stick out my tongue?

"Word to the wise, ma'am. You'll want to turn around now and skedaddle. He's an unscrupulous con man. Woman like you deserves better."

And I planned on having better. But that was none of Fat Monkey's business. I said nothing, but my mind was already working on all the pieces of the puzzle he'd just handed me.

He tipped his nonexistent hat again, and the window eased back up. I watched as the van slid down the driveway. Like a snake crossing a grassy field after ruining the picnic of my life.

21

Needless to say, I did not take the fat stranger's advice. But I did stash the no-kick champagne in the trunk of my car. Due to the day's complicating information, I decided to postpone the big announcement until a later date. The mood was decidedly ruined anyway, and I would not be staying long. No sex either. My man might notice the mildly thickened swelling at my waist and figure it out on his own, and that wasn't part of the plan.

On the way to the front door, I was in an altered state. My body moved ahead while my mind operated on overdrive. The two thugs from Jersey, their boss demanding his money. I needed to find out what that was all about without allowing my fiancé to postpone the wedding date. I also had to keep his hands and eyes off my belly until I could determine it was safe to make the announcement. All of this would be challenging.

What I needed was a drink.

As I entered the foyer, I heard voices from the stairs to the second-floor bedrooms. Mojito. With Greta right behind him. Both kids dressed in skimpy bathing suits. A couple of smiling, happy teenagers.

I sped through the living room on my way to the sliding glass doors. Stay cool, I told myself. Ignore him and focus on your fiancé. First Mojito, then second Mojito.

"Hey, teach," my young love sang out. "Wait for us." He caught up, said in a low voice, "You'll want to take it slow today. Dad's just finished having it out with some nasty investors."

Nasty *investors*?

Ping. Everything clicked into place. Mr. Mojito was another Bernie, all right. But not Bernie Sanders. The other Bernie. Bernard Madoff, the world's most successful investment con man.

I felt my mouth drop open. Time seemed to halt as the puzzle pieces rearranged themselves and the full picture formed in my mind. Oh God, oh God. The game had changed right before my eyes.

I must have looked distraught because Mojito stopped smiling and searched my face. "You okay?"

Greta came up behind him, putting a slim hand on his bare shoulder. Possessively, I thought. "You need a glass of water?" she asked.

She was sweet, I had to admit. I couldn't despise the girl if I wanted to, which I did.

Instantly, I snapped out of it. "You two surprised me, that's all. I'm fine." Fake smile, little phony laugh. While inside me, something had died.

Not the baby. No, I think what I felt was the final gasp of my wonderful, brilliant, romantic fantasy. My plan for my future. Mine and Mojito's. Although I didn't know that then. Not yet.

They moved as if to pass by me but I stood there, blocking their way. "Is your dad really upset? I mean, you think he needs time alone?" I was fishing. Trying to prepare my game. Because the roles had flipped and now I was on the hook. "Should we bring out a bottle of wine? Or something stronger?"

I was trying to get Mojito alone so I could ask him some other questions. Continue to build the puzzle with additional pieces.

"Probably. You know where the wine is. Grab him a bottle."

I looked at Mojito. Why was he treating me this way? Did he think it was okay to boss me around like that in front of someone? Then I glanced at her. She was staring up at him, her emerald eyes shining with admiration.

Oh.

"Gotcha. Will do," I said. "But you need to come with me to the wine cellar and select something. I don't know the difference between a Château five thousand dollars and a Publix special."

I chuckled, but what I meant was, *Send her on her way, we need to talk.*

He shook his head. Not going to happen. "So bring out a bottle of single malt. He'll appreciate that."

They eased past me, smelling of suntan lotion and something else. Weed. And, yes, sex.

My heart hurt. I actually put one hand to my chest, covering the wound. Stanching the bleeding.

As I wandered down the hall to the dining room to fetch some kind of medicinal booze, my mind raced ahead. Oh my god, I'd conned a con man! Here I was, all ready to marry him for his money, but his wealth belonged to other people. And, from the looks of it, unsavory people. Maybe angry, ready to wring necks, break legs, and put two in the back of the head kind of people.

I walked slowly, thinking it through. I'd never overheard my fiancé on a business call nor met any of his business peers. His work life was vague, but that seemed natural. I'd thought of it as a rich man's hobby. But now I saw things differently. Fake company, fake background, fake hedge fund, fake earnings. And how many unsatisfied investors were out there? I doubted the list was confined to the Monkey Family from Jersey. For all the wealth Mr. Mojito flaunted, there would have to be an awful lot of rich folks who'd trusted him with their money. Dirty or clean, he had taken it all. And done what with it, I wondered.

The maid was vacuuming the Persian carpet in my fiancé's home office. I walked by, then wandered back. When she noticed me standing in the doorway, she snapped off the loud machine, dragged it from the room. A tiny woman with close-cropped gray hair, she had never uttered a single word to me. I figured she didn't speak English. She looked like she might be from the islands, or maybe South America.

I walked in the office and shut the door behind me. The blinds were drawn, and the overly air-conditioned room was cold and dark. I moved to the antique desk, switched on a small lamp. My heart pounding hard and fast, I opened each of the four desk drawers, hunting. For what, I wasn't sure. Any information that might give me a hint about what the hell to do next would be helpful. But there was nothing. Pens, breath mints, bills. Fliers, notepads, change. Paperclips, condoms. A sketchpad with blank pages. A fifth of Jack Daniels.

I closed all the drawers. What I needed to know had to be on his computer.

I flipped open the laptop and keyed in the first password I thought of. Mojito, and the numbers for his birth date.

Nothing.

Then I typed in my fiancé's name and birth date. Nope. Then mine: Cathriona, my birth date. Nothing. I tried Cathriona and our wedding date.

Bingo.

This made me sad. And so confused I closed the lid. I stood there, still leaning over his desk, stunned. He actually loved me? I mean, why else would he use my name and our wedding date for his password?

I shut off the light and felt my way across the dark room to the door. Nobody out in the hall. I walked quickly to the dining room and over to the wet bar. My heart pounded in my ears like a hangover headache. I needed to calm down before I went outside to my fiancé. He couldn't see me jacked up like this. It wasn't time to play my hand. I didn't even know what my next move would be. Not anymore.

After I located the right size tumbler, I poured myself three fingers of Clase Azul top-shelf tequila.

Boom.

I stood there in a daze. Sunlight flooded the tall windows and bounced off the long mahogany dining table, the ten upholstered high-back chairs. I was confused, nervous, sad, scared, my heart kicking around in my chest like an aimless child. I didn't know what to do or whom to trust. I couldn't even trust myself. Least of all myself.

Finally taking my shattered self in hand, I grabbed a bottle of Corzo and two clean glasses. As I walked down the hall to the living room, I weighed my options. Convince Mojito to run off with me, have the baby, and live together in love and poverty? Pathetic. Go ahead with the wedding in the face of possible serious consequences from my husband's questionable business dealings? Scary. Convince him to sign the prenup he was so adamantly against instituting? Perhaps his reasoning for this was not as romantic as he claimed. Did he plan to leave me, his wife, holding the empty bag? Maybe my best option was to withdraw from the situation. But was I willing to lose my Mojito? To possibly give up the boy forever?

Oh no. No, no, no.

I stood by the sliders, trying to slow my pulse. I swallowed hard, my mouth dry, so dry. The adrenaline charged around my body, leaving behind fiery little balls of anxiety. Calm, Cath, calm. Get a grip, you still need to play the dedicated lover. Run your lines now, then deal with the reality later, I told myself in a sensible inner voice. When the time was right, I could check his computer. Find out what was going on. Then make my decision. My new plan.

The game had changed, but it was not over yet.

I slid open the door and stepped onto the brick pavers, then headed for the pool deck. The sun had dropped lower in the sky, dusk fast approaching. Dwindling light glimmered on the Intracoastal and clean white boats splashed through it. A songbird whistled from a tree branch overhead.

A mockingbird. How appropriate.

The kids were lying on their stomachs on matching sea-green air mattresses, floating head to head. Sleek and wet, chins on hands, they looked into one another's eyes. I stood there staring, more alone than ever before.

"Cath!"

My fiancé waved to me from the garden, his face somber. I tore my eyes from the teenage love fest and walked over. The bright yellow, pink, and red hibiscus bragged of buoyant fertility. I felt soiled.

After kissing the top of his head, I set the bottle and glasses on the table. Next to a half-empty bottle of Scotch and two glasses with melted ice.

"You had company?" I asked innocently, sitting down in the chair across from him. I angled it carefully so I could watch the pool. "Or are you drinking for two today?"

I kept my voice teasing and light. I scanned his face but he gave me nothing. In fact, he smiled gently at me. Like a patient man with his darling doltish girlfriend.

"Just a client from out of town," he said dismissively.

End of discussion.

He raised a brow, tilted his head toward the house. As if to say, *Upstairs to bed, darling?*

I pretended not to catch this. I wanted to watch Mojito. See if he would eye me lustily while he toyed with Greta. Give me an indication he was still, always, mine. And I was going to make this visit short, while keeping my blustery midriff covered at all times.

"I'm in the mood for shots of tequila." The party girl face in place, I poured us each a generous serving. I'd forgotten the salt, the limes. Oh well. Bottoms up.

He frowned. "Sorry. I'm not in the mood today."

If things hadn't turned upside down, that would have been my line. No booze for *our* baby! As it was, I knew my substitute line so I poured another shot, then said it. "What *are* you in the mood for, darling?"

He leaned across the table, taking a breast in each cool hand. "Comfort, baby. Comfort."

I smiled. A fake loving smile. He leaned in farther, kissed me passionately. His tongue tasted of malt. And acid. Ash.

After a long and rather fervent kiss, he stood. He waited, looking down at me. His lust, his desire, all there for me. Just me.

When he held out a hand, I took it. He pulled me up, wrapped an arm around my shoulders, and led me toward the house. I had no choice. The heart wants what the heart wants.

His, not mine.

The sun was going down fast but the pinkish daylight lingered. It would not be dark in the master bedroom. Not dark enough anyway. How would I hide my belly? How could I take off my clothes and spread myself open without my lover seeing my secret? Who was this man, and what had he done? What did he want with me? What did *I* want? Everything swirled around in my head and, along with the two glasses of tequila, sunk fast to boil painfully in my gut.

On our way across the pool deck, I glanced down at the youngsters floating in the pool. They were gazing at each other languidly. Talking in whispery voices, ignoring the adults. When Mojito reached for her bare shoulder, stroking it with his long fingers, my insides screamed out.

Burn, heart, burn.

It burned worse than any Mexican tequila. Way worse.

22

The bedroom was semi-dark and cool, his lovemaking fierce. Mr. Mojito came at me like he was starved for it. Maybe that's what worked in my favor because he took me right away without stopping to remove my clothes and observe my naked body. He just bent me over the edge of his king-size bed, pulled up my skirt, and had at it. He clutched my hips the whole time, his mind on his own pleasure. His own immediate gratification.

I groaned. Oh my god, how every woman loves a fascist.

After he was done, he kissed my sweaty neck and crawled onto the bed, fell asleep without a word. I stared at him in the dimming light. More gray hair around the temples, deeper furrows in the brow. Who was this old man? And what exactly was he getting me involved in?

I mopped up in the vast and gilded bathroom, not bothering to shower. I needed to head home before he awoke and return when he was out. That was my only plan at the moment and I was determined to stick with it.

He let out a piggish snore when I tiptoed past. Drunk, or just aged? Either way, I felt nothing. I had almost cared for him. Now I would always feel nothing.

Out front, Mojito's BMW was gone. When I opened my car door, a folded piece of notepaper sat on the driver's seat. *You make Daddy happy, Dr. O?*

I texted Mojito, waited. No response.

Then I felt everything. And it all felt bad.

The next day during my lunch hour, I left school and drove to the Mojitos' house. I parked next door in a sandy half-acre lot where construction would soon be underway. Yet another McMansion going up on a stripped-down wedge of waterfront gold.

I walked across the beach grass to the water's edge, then made my way through the overgrowth that separated the empty lot from my lovers' property. Spiky bougainvillea scratched at my arms, knifelike sawgrass nicked my legs. Mother Nature had her ways of being cruel. Or maybe she was just self-protective.

Clytemnestra rocked on the choppy water, occasionally rubbing herself against the dock like a needy cat. The yard was empty, lustrous in the afternoon light. I hurried up the lawn to the side yard, then cut through to the front of the house. I wasn't out of breath but my blood zinged around my body and the adrenaline pumped good and hard.

No cars were parked in the driveway. If the maid stopped me inside, I would say I was there to retrieve my wallet. Or my panties. I'd think of something. Hey, I was the bride-to-be. I had a right to be in my fiancé's mansion.

I let myself in and headed straight for his office. The house was bright and warm, which was strange. Usually it was like walking into an igloo.

The office door was closed. I opened it, slipped inside, and shut the door behind me. The room was dark, but not cool. In fact, it felt stuffy. Whatever, I wouldn't be there long. Still, I was sweating as I sat down at the desk. The swivel chair was made of cushiony leather. I rolled to a stop and listened for sounds coming from the rest of the house.

Nothing. It was so quiet I could hear the ticking of a chunky Rolex my fiancé had left on the desk, right next to his computer. I picked up the watch. A heavy gold with Roman numerals, it probably cost in the five figures. Unless it was a fake? I examined it closely, my funhouse-mirror face reflected in the smooth metal band. How would I be able to tell?

Setting it back where I found it, I popped open the laptop and went to work. File after file, click and skim. There was one labeled *My Poetry*. I opened it, read some of the poems. I was wildly impressed until I recognized a few lines from Rossetti.

Had he been passing off others' work as his own? Now that's low, stealing from dead poets. What a cheat! I so hate plagiarism. Do your own work, people. Writing is extraordinarily hard, and most writers make very little money. Not fair ripping them off!

I calmed myself, kept skimming his files. And suddenly, there it was. *Boom.* The aha moment. Oh my god.

I shut the lid and sat there for a minute, stunned.

In a daze, I left the office and walked down the hall. The unmistakable roar of a vacuum came from upstairs. Was that all the sullen maid ever did? She didn't serve meals, fetch wine, bring out pots of coffee, or make herself available to answer the door. Not to my knowledge. When I thought about it, she was as mysterious as her boss.

Although I now had a better handle on who Mr. Mojito really was. What he was about. And how I fit into his playbook. This new information was unsettling, to say the least.

Not bothering to be quiet, I let myself out the sliding glass doors, strolling down the back lawn. I had every right to be there. When the hairs on the top of my head prickled, I turned around. Sure enough, the maid stood out on the patio, staring at me. I waved, but she did not.

Less than twenty minutes later, I parked my car in the school lot. Armed with the new intel, a whole new plan was forming in my mind. What did I feel then? Oh God, oh God, I felt hopeful.

That night I met my fiancé for dinner at a way-too-hip bistro in downtown Delray Beach. We sat out front on the crowded patio. Our fellow diners were dressed in their finest designer garb. Heavy Rolexes glimmered, blobby diamonds glittered. Teeth flashed, and everyone showed off the latest in plastic enhancements.

After our unfriendly young waitress poured the wine, my lover took my hand, kissed it. Then he said we needed to get married sooner than we'd planned. He didn't tell me why. In fact, all he said was this: "I moved the wedding up to a week from Saturday. Now don't say no, Cathriona. I insist."

I sipped the Barbaresco. Full bodied, aromatic, and sure to bring on a massive next-day headache. I thought about telling him I wasn't ready. But my protruding belly was telling me to shut up. Give in. Get on with the show.

I fake smiled. "Whatever you want, darling."

He leaned in for a proper kiss. "You. All I want is you," he said, his handsome face sincere.

Or was it?

I kissed him back but, for the first time since meeting the charming Mr. Mojito, I doubted his sincerity. I didn't let on, of course. We remained liplocked, clinging to each other like a couple of teenagers. The whole restaurant saw us. Which was, of course, the point. *His* point. And mine as well.

When we finally pulled apart, I said, "And all *I* want is you, darling."

He stroked my carefully arranged face, I stared deep in his lying eyes. The perfect couple.

We continued to pet and perform throughout the meal. After the waitress served me a steaming espresso, however, he said he had to go. He had a "meeting with a client."

At ten o'clock at night? Right.

But I nodded, agreeable as always. "I'll stay for a bit and enjoy my coffee. I need the caffeine. I have a huge pile of term papers to grade." A lie, of course. Anything to avoid the boudoir and hide my midriff bulge.

He smiled at what he thought was my passive attitude, my unquestioning acceptance. Oh yes, I thought with a surge of pride, two could play at his game. Apparently, two had been playing all along.

He stood. I stared at this stranger, my lover, possibly the father of my unborn child. My heart did not lift, neither did it dance. When he leaned down and kissed me goodbye, I closed my eyes, inhaling the garlic on his breath, the metallic smell of his nervous sweat. He was either afraid of me or, more likely, whomever he was meeting in the darkness.

After he left, I sat for a while. Sipping the rich coffee, I watched the street absentmindedly as sleek car after luxury car slid by and disappeared over the bridge to the ocean. It was a beautiful night, not too hot, not too hectic. I could feel the slow days of summer approaching. I sighed, enjoying the idle moment. I so wished I could dial my life back to the not-so-distant past in which I was simply a lonely English teacher who took on the occasional inappropriate lover.

But then I would not have Mojito. And Mojito was everything. My everything.

. . .

On my way home, I reworked the plan in my mind. I would have to accommodate my fiancé's shortened timetable. I had to work around the lack of a prenup, which complicated things for me and, ultimately, for Mojito. We didn't want to end up paying the consequences for his father's financial indiscretions. That would be no way for us to launch a life together. We might not even survive.

Things moved very fast after that. The reception invitations were E-mailed, a local caterer and a party band booked. Soon enough everything was all lined up like the cute little diamonds on the engagement ring my fiancé gave me.

I had the gems checked at a franchise jeweler's at the mall. As expected, zircon. I was emotionally prepared for that, but still, it hurt.

By this time, few of my clothes fit properly. I bought a half-dozen flouncy blouses and spoke often about how I needed to shed some pounds if I was going to get into my wedding dress. The women at work were supportive, suggesting grapefruit diets, juice fasts and the like.

My true love ignored me. Mojito and Greta were an item at school and an absence at the house. Just as well. Unlike his father, Mojito would have been able to read in my face that something inside me had changed. I didn't want him to know what I had found out about his father until I was ready to tell him.

There was no bridal shower. I didn't have close friends like that. I hadn't invited my relatives to the reception either. Hugh was not on the guest list, of course, since my fiancé did not know I had a brother. So none of the Florida west coast clan would be in attendance. But, just to make it look like I was trying, I'd added a dozen names to the reception list. Teachers, secretaries, and kids from school. A few of the lit profs I had known at FBU. Tina, my hairstylist. A nice bartender from one of the beach bars and her accountant husband.

There was no rehearsal dinner. The ceremony was going to be small, simple, very private. Just us, Mojito and Greta, a local notary. Or so my fiancé informed me. I barely listened, the plan changed so often. Whatever, I just wanted to get it done. Mrs. Mojito, one two three.

The day before the wedding, torrential rain fell from the sky like a biblical warning. I mean I took it as a sign from the gods. My fiancé had not made love to me since the day I had overheard him arguing with the Jersey thugs. Mojito was no longer communicating with me by text, phone, or anything else. I was several months into a pregnancy I didn't want. And I was about to marry the wrong man.

Maybe that's why I poured a shot of tequila in my morning coffee. Maybe that's why I spent the next half hour in the bathroom, throwing up. When I looked at myself in the mirror over the sink, I did not look like a happy bride. My eyes were bloodshot, my hair knotted and damp with sweat. My face seemed a little yellow. As a matter of fact, I looked like an alcoholic. An old bottle hag.

Maybe because I was one.

I brushed my teeth, splashed water on my face, and smoothed my skin with after-sun coconut crème. I had to get going. I had an appointment at Tipsy Tina's to get my hair done.

When I walked into the chic chrome and glass salon, Tina greeted me with a wink and a champagne glass full of bubbles.

"Big day tomorrow, Cathriona. You'll need a bit of the old liquid courage."

An extraordinarily tall woman with a deep voice and a conspicuous Adam's apple, Tina was the best stylist I'd ever had the luck to encounter. She snipped a bit here, added some highlights there, and *voila*: I looked years younger.

Plus, she served drinks.

We were alone in the small salon. The other two swivel chairs were empty. As always, the air reeked of perfumed hair products that made my eyes smart.

Tina tsked and clucked as she worked on my stubborn snarls with a wide comb. "Whatever have you been doing with that man? He been pulling you by the hair, dragging you into his man cave?" She laughed her rumbling he-man's chuckle.

Ha ha.

After she combed out the tangles and set me up for a wash, she said, "Darlin', I've prepped a lot of brides in my time in this business. Fat brides, ugly brides, shotgun brides, virginal scared-to-death brides. And sweetheart, you look like the worst of the lot." She massaged my scalp with her big man's hands. "I don't understand you, Cathriona. You're marrying a prince, a man who can give you everything. Man has money, looks, maturity, money. Did I mention money? What's *wrong* with you, girlfriend?"

I didn't say anything. I was trying too hard not to barf.

"If I had a man like that in my bed? At our age? I'd be down on my knees praying to the Lord. And I'm a fucking atheist," she said between rinses.

That made me laugh.

After she sat me upright again, a fluffy towel wrapped around my head, I carefully avoided looking at myself in the mirror. Without my thick head of youthful hair to disguise the truth, I looked like an old lady. When my hair was wet, I could see the ugly crone everyone would see in the not-too-distant future.

Still, the sobs surprised me. They came out of nowhere.

The next thing I knew, Tina had her wiry arms around me and I was weeping against her hard breasts. She patted my back gently, said, *there there*, and *let it all out, sweetheart.*

When the weeping finally spent itself, she asked if I needed a refill on my drink. Then she went to get one for me without waiting for an answer.

Later, when we were allowing the color to set, she asked, "You gonna keep it?"

I stared at her sharp features, her piercing black eyes. She was smart, and solid. Almost a friend. "What would you do?" I asked, sipping at the champagne.

"Honey, the day I turn the stick blue will be the day the good Lord's only son has come down to scoop me up, make love to me himself."

"I thought the same thing," I told her. "I'm forty-two."

Of course, I took a few years off. Okay, more than a few. Still, this was about as close to my real age as I ever admitted. And I had yet to do one of those home tests. I already knew what the results would be. No lying to myself about that one. Baby on the way.

Tina kept at my hair.

After a few silent minutes, during which she took years off my face with her styling magic, she said, "I know a doctor. He's good. Real careful. Discreet."

I didn't say anything. I didn't have to.

When she was done, my hair looked fantastic. Highlighted with streaks of gold, swept off my face, hanging down my back in a silky curtain. I looked a good ten years younger than when I'd arrived. I tipped her lavishly.

She took my phone, keyed in a name and number. "In case you make a decision," she said.

After we hugged, I said, "You're a lifesaver. See you tomorrow."

She patted my face. "Look on the bright side, sugar. He loves you. The rest is bath water. You can throw that out too."

I smiled as if I agreed. But of course that wasn't what I thought. Not at all.

23

Ladies and gentlemen, you've been amazingly patient with me up to this point in my discourse. You've withheld judgment regarding my irresponsible behavior, the perverse crush on a student, the excessive drinking—even while pregnant, and the sluttish lovemaking with two partners. Two closely related partners. For this, your open-minded interest in my sordid story, I thank you. But now I must warn you about what comes next. It does not make me look good. So please, open your mind even further, and your heart as well. Because you must trust me on this: soon enough, once I finish telling you my story, you will slide right on over to my side of the church.

That day before my wedding, when I drove home from Tipsy Tina's, I had only one thing on my mind: Mojito. If I focused on the future we would soon have together, stepmother and stepson living side by side and loving one another truly madly deeply, I could convince myself everything I planned on doing to make this happen was right. All good, in fact. I was convinced this was still the best option available to me. To us.

But when I thought about the wedding and the days and nights to follow that singular (in my life, at least) event, my heart sputtered and the bile raced up my throat. Because there would be such obstacles, such dangers involved in bringing the future I wanted to fruition. All of it, the conniving, the lying, the danger, the chance of bloodshed, just thinking about it made me physically sick.

I drove slowly. The rain had ceased for the moment but the sky still threatened. The humidity was not good for my hairdo, so I kept the windows up, the AC on high. At the next red light, I checked my phone. Several texts from Mr. Mojito. He was making sure I had picked up my dress from the shop where I'd had it altered. Looser in front, less clingy, thank you. Another text to tell me he'd added several people to the guest list. Last-minute additions were still allowed. Was I sure none of my relatives could make it? He would fly them in on a client's private jet if they wanted to join us.

Thank you, darling, so sweet, I texted back before the light changed.

He was, really, especially considering the lies I'd been telling him in this regard. He thought my relatives disapproved of him, an older divorced man with a kid. In truth, anyone who knew me well would have been ecstatic to hear I was about to wed an actual adult. I was not about to explain any of this, however. Not to my husband-to-be.

Hugh had washed his hands of me years before. The last time I saw my dear brother was at our parents' double funeral. I thought it was tacky to have both caskets at the front of the visiting room. They should have been given separate rooms many years earlier. Maybe that could have prevented their final disaster.

Hugh took my comments on the matter badly. "The only thing they ever fought about was you," he said in a low voice as the solemn guests filtered past us to stop for a moment by each coffin. My brother's heavy black suit was tight all over. He'd gained weight and seemed as miserable as our dad had been. "Your sick escapades ruined their marriage."

I shrugged. "Blame me, if it makes you feel better. But all they ever gave me was a cold shoulder."

His beefy face turned a deeper shade of red. "Bullshit, Cath. They rescued your crazy ass dozens of times. And worried constantly about what you'd do next. You should've been locked up. You're fucking pathological. It makes me sick to think of how you ruined our family."

I patted his meaty shoulder. "Good news. This is the very last time you will have to put up with me, bro."

And I had been true to my word.

After I parked in my space under the green canopy, I checked my hair in the rearview. Still smooth as autumn velveteen. I faked a smile. Not young looking, but youth-full. It would have to do.

I opened my door and stepped out. And there he was, coming right at me. In worn jeans and a soft yellow T-shirt. His face somber, but boyish, and so beautiful.

Mojito. Mo-hee-toe. My heart lurched around like a drunken fool.

I shut the car door, walked past him. "Go home. We can't be seen together, not today."

He grabbed my shoulder, pulled me to him in a bearish hug. He smelled freshly salted, like the sea. When I tried to push him away, he held me tight, whispered hoarsely, "I can do what I want, Cath. And what I want is you."

One Mojito, two Mojito. Which one was a liar, I wondered, and who was telling the truth?

"If you really want me, you'll get in your car and go home. Or go to Greta's. Wherever. If you don't, you're going to ruin it. You'll ruin everything." My voice was crushed flat against the taut muscles covering his breastbone. His heart was in there, beating steadily. "I want you too. You know that. Just not now."

He let me go. His eyes looked as stormy as the sky overhead. It had begun to drizzle. My hair would be ruined.

I hurried off, heading for the side entrance to my building. I was hoping he would do what I'd asked. But he didn't. He grabbed the door after I unlocked it, held it open for me, then followed me inside.

"If you're going to insist, the least you can do is be discreet. Don't make a scene. Wait here for a few minutes, then come up. I'll leave the door open."

But he was right behind me when I started up the stairs. I wasn't about to go out to the lobby and take the elevator. Not with a student tagging along. What if someone saw us?

The stairwell was empty, dark and dingy. As I hustled up the cement steps ahead of him, he pushed past me. Waiting at the next landing, he grabbed me, pinned me to the wall. Through the thin fabric of my cotton blouse, the cement felt cold and rough. He kissed me hard, and soon enough I heard the stutter of an unzipping fly.

I turned my head, pulling my mouth from his. "Don't. Are you crazy?"

I pushed at his arms, but he didn't budge. He dragged his hot mouth to my breasts, sucking at them through my shirt. I shoved his head away. He yanked up my skirt, sliding his fingers inside me. Of course, there he found the telltale signs of my desire. I couldn't hide that, not from Mojito.

If you saw the video, you would know the sex was consensual. Even if he looked aggressive in the beginning, by the time we were done I was as guilty of satiating a greedy lust as the boy was.

Up against the wall in a dirty stairwell. Less than twenty-four hours before getting married. To his father, no less. What a pair. Obviously, we were perfect for one another, Mojito and I.

The look he gave me when he left me there in the stairwell, panting, dripping with his fertile seed, is something I will never forget. The combination of his intense desire and bitter anger made my heart skitter and sink. Oh, Mojito. All we needed was a little more patience, and trust in our love. Didn't you see what you could do to me?

Straightening my clothing, I got myself together enough to venture out to the hallway. Nobody there, thank God. I dashed down the hall, almost weeping with fear and elation. Safe inside my apartment, I poured myself a big glass of tequila. Then I fed the circling cats. After that, I went to the bathroom to check on my hair.

My eyes were haunted, my hair still lovely. It would have to do.

When my phone went, I thought it might be him. Begging me not to marry his father. Insisting there had to be another way. For a moment, my heart unlocked its bone cage and peered out.

But it wasn't Mojito. It was his father. A door inside me slammed shut.

I let the call go, poured myself another drink. And soon after that, another.

Out on the balcony, I sat looking at the sky. Afternoon slid into evening, dusk to dark. For hours, I ran the tape loop in my mind of our sexual interlude. The boy was crazed with desire. Such an insane passion. I could never let that go. Never.

The phone kept going. Mr. Mojito, again and again. Wasn't it bad luck for the bride and groom to speak on the night before the wedding?

Just in case, I refused to take his calls.

I crawled onto my bed at some point, and passed out.

. . .

When I awoke, it was dark and my head felt like an anvil. An invisible hammer was pounding on it. *Bang, bang, bang.* Then I remembered my hair.

I got up fast, so fast the room spun. I moved carefully to the bathroom mirror. Magically, my hair looked fine. With a few pats here and there, it appeared just as it had when Tina finished with it. The girl was a wizard. I owed her.

I leaned in. My eyes weren't bad either. Possibly because I'd had quite a few hours of sleep. Except for the dynamite blasts in my head, I felt good. Clean minded and full of energy.

Which was a surprise and a relief, because I would need it. The day would require a perfect performance on my part. The blushing bride. The happy newlywed. The ecstatic wife. I had to pull that off without any slipups.

Which meant no drinking.

The funhouse mirror warbled then, and I morphed into a yellow-faced alcoholic with wild gray hair and no teeth. Behind my witchy head, the room resembled a cage. Or a prison cell.

I turned away and erased the image from my mind. Then I ran a hot shower and steamed up the mirror. No time for lunacy, I needed to prepare myself for my wedding day.

By the time I finished the third cup of double-strength coffee, the day had dawned hot and bright. No more rain, not a cloud in the baby-blue sky.

I felt cleaned out, fresh, and on top of my game. I was ready for my new life. After the honeymoon, I would move to the Mojitos' place. My condo would serve as my own private writing retreat. My fiancé had advised me to keep it for this purpose. In fact, he suggested I stop writing short fiction and instead devote myself to a novel. A saga full of lust and lies. "You'd enjoy it," he'd told me several times. "Being a novelist suits your personality."

I wasn't sure what he meant. That I was an introvert? A creative? A storyteller? My fiction had repeatedly failed to interest anyone beyond myself. So I had turned away from stories to focus purely on journaling. If my husband-to-be had known that all I wrote about was my burning desire for his son, for Mojito, he might not have encouraged me to keep my condo and pursue my writing life.

Or maybe that was all part of his plan. The one he didn't share with me.

At seven, I texted him. Asked if he'd been able to get any sleep. Told him it would have been bad luck if we'd talked the previous night. Included two smiley faces and a kiss-lips.

He did not respond.

The ceremony was scheduled for eleven. I drank more coffee, then called my fiancé again. The iceberg floating in my tropical sea of paradise.

No answer.

I texted Mojito. *Where's your dad?*

He texted back. *Waiting for you. At the house.*

I felt like I was living in a cartoon. The furniture was on the ceiling.

After I hunted down an overnight bag, I packed for the wedding night. New lingerie. Perfume. Sex toys. The thermos I used for a flask. I planned to remain sober before and during the wedding, but after would be a different story. Or maybe it would be my usual story, but told to my new husband instead.

I dressed and accessorized. The dress was a cream-colored sheath with flounces in all the right places, and it fit perfectly. No bumps showed, baby or otherwise. A classic pair of Manolo

Blahniks. Blue drop earrings with real sapphires, the new engagement ring with its phony stones. And a delicate gold chain bracelet my grandmother had given my mother on her wedding day.

My grandmother had been as chilly as her daughter, my dearly departed ice queen mother. But they both had exquisite taste. Too bad I'd been forced to sell off so much of the inherited jewelry, their silver and china, the antiques. But a girl has to live, doesn't she. I had lived quite well on others' spoils. Now I would marry a man who did the same. Who would be the spoiler, and who the spoiled?

In the full-length mirror, I scanned the final results. I cocked my head, my hair a shimmering strawberry hue in the morning light. Oh yes, I was rooting for youth. I was always rooting for youth. No matter what Hugh said, my parents' coldness had frozen something in me. The blood still fed the infection. And the wound wouldn't heal. Mojito was warm balm for that icy scar. He was the only cure for my frigid soul.

With a sigh, I took one last look at myself. A beautiful bride? Not exactly, but I did look good. At least ten years younger than my real age. Sadly, this was probably as good as I was going to get. Ever. The rapid slide downhill had already begun, so everything was only going to look worse and worse after this. Mother Nature being such a bitch.

After texting my unresponsive groom that I was on my way, I popped my phone in the clutch that matched my dress and shoes, and bid my two kitties goodbye. "Don't be so nasty, Zora. You're looking at me like I have two heads."

The big black cat yawned, then sat down and licked her crotch.

"Nice one, Z."

I blew a kiss to my sweet gray Pearl, who slunk past, meowing softly.

As ready as I'd ever be, I grabbed my overnight bag and headed for the elevator. Nobody in the hall, as usual. No one to stare at me in my bridal outfit.

I waited for the elevator, trying not to sweat. I wasn't nervous, but I knew that would come soon enough. When I had to face all Mr. Mojito's friends and clients, and act as if today was the most important day of my life.

I certainly hoped it was not.

The elevator dinged and the brass doors slid open. To my dismay, there was a boy in the elevator. A gangly boy dressed in a drab brown uniform. Building security.

He pushed the button to keep the doors open, insisted on helping me with my overnight bag. His skinny face was acne scarred, his fingernails bitten to the quick. I like boys but only the ones who resemble movie stars' kids. This one looked like one of my junk-food students bussed in from the Everglades.

After I thanked the kid, he stared at me, his eyes bold, laughing. What, did I look funny to him? I looked down at my beautiful shoes, embarrassed.

"Hey," he said after more rude gawking. We stood side by side, watching the numbers go down. "You marrying your boyfriend?"

No. Not exactly. I'm marrying into his family. Best I can do. For now.

I didn't say that, of course. I said, "Do I look like a bride to you?" Kind of sharp, but his snarky tone was contagious.

He snickered. "You sure didn't look like one yesterday."

What *was* he talking about? Had I bumped into him in the hall after drinking all that tequila? But I hadn't left the balcony, not that I recalled. And by eight o'clock, I'd stumbled straight to bed.

When the elevator jerked to a stop and dinged, this time *I* pressed the stop button to keep the doors closed. "Okay, buddy.

What are you on about?" I tried to sound good-humored, but I felt like slapping his smug face. "You apparently have something you're just dying to say to me."

He grinned. His teeth needed straightening. And brushing. "Next time you see your boyfriend, the guy around my age? You can tell him this building's wired for security. Cameras everywhere. Including..." He paused, looked me up and down. "...the stairwells."

Oh God, oh God.

When he reached to press the open doors button, his gnawed hand brushed against the front of my dress. I jumped back, and he let out a chuckle. Then he stepped off the elevator and walked away, a goofy swagger to his step. The scrawny bastard. I waited a moment, writhing in humiliation.

Like I said, if you saw the security video, you would know our sex that day was consensual. The security creep had just confirmed it.

And, in about an hour, I would be marrying my stairwell lover's dad.

With an allover body shiver, I hoisted my little suitcase and slunk out to the parking lot.

24

The driveway was crowded with top-of-the-line cars. I pulled in behind a silver Lamborghini and in front of a classic 1969 Mustang, cream colored with red leather seats. My groom must have invited some of the reception guests to come early. I checked my phone. The notary was due any minute.

A sunburned kid claiming to be the valet asked for my key, told me he'd be sure to take good care of my shitbox car. He didn't actually say that, but there was an amused gleam in his eyes. Obviously, he was going to hide it somewhere out of view, keep showing off the luxury vehicles. I handed him the key with a frown. God knows, I'd had enough of brash teenagers to last me for a while.

Wasn't I supposed to make a grand entrance? No chance of that. I walked carefully up the slick marble steps and into the foyer, lugging my overnight bag. Not romantic in the least.

Inside, strangers milled around the living room, filling it with a sound I'd never heard before in that house. The sound of a large gathering of people. Everyone seemed to be laughing, talking, having a good time. Outside in the garden, across the lawn and on the pool deck, more joyful people. Many held coffee cups. Some munched on pastries.

Was I expected to entertain these folks until the ceremony began? I was not up for that. No meet and greet for me until after I officially became the new Mrs. Mojito. At least, this was how I had imagined the day: a private exchange of vows, then the party. Apparently, my husband-to-be had other ideas on the itinerary for the day.

Needless to say, what I wanted was a drink. I would wait upstairs with maybe a genteel and unaromatic V&T. Check my face, relax, get ready for the I dos.

I ducked down the hall to the dining room. But the maid was in there, standing by the wet bar. Alone, silent and dark as ever. I stopped in the doorway and stared at her. She wasn't cleaning or mixing the guests' drinks. She was drinking, working on a tumbler of something or other, with an extra grim expression on her normally grim face.

I walked over and set my bag on the bar. "That looks good. Bourbon?"

She gave me the stink eye, her lips unmoving, her body language telling me everything. She hated me. In fact, she was seething with disgust, distaste, vitriol.

Not the best time to pour myself a stiff one, I decided. I pretended I was there to stow my gear. Leaning past her to tuck my bag behind the bar, I said, "Where's the groom hiding himself?"

This was the first time she'd ever looked me in the eye. She bared a set of grayish teeth. When she spoke, her accent was thick, her words like stones hitting my face. "You don't know, you know nothing. *Nada*. You know nothing 'bout anything. You make with the boy, you make with the father, you break two hearts. But still, you go on. You, you, all 'bout you. Ha. You know nothing. *Nada, niña estùpida*. Stupid girl."

With that, she spat on me. A bourbon-flavored hock of spittle hit my lips and chin, splattering down my neck, dripping onto the front of my dress. She picked up her drink and stormed off.

I stood there trying to recover my cool. It wasn't easy.

What was *with* everyone today? Did I have a target on my forehead that said, *Piss on me*?

Resisting a beseeching urge to do a couple of nerve-strengthening shots of hundred-proof anything, I tore myself away from the bar. After blotting my face and neck with a cloth napkin from the breakfront, I left the empty room in search of my future hubby.

First order from the new wife: fire the maid.

I spotted Mojito. He stood out, a neon sign calling me into the garden. The roses too were ablaze, and everything bloomed around him. But he was even more dazzling than the flora, dressed in white slacks and a white form-fitting jacket. His gorgeous tanned face, the long shiny hair, the morning sun lighting up the sleek linen suit. My lord.

When he looked up and saw me coming, however, his face shifted.

One long arm rested lightly around Greta's pencil-thin waist. She was wrapped in pale-green spandex that fit her like a surgeon's glove. A dress better suited for clubbing, I thought. But she was my maid of honor, and beggars can't choose much of anything, so I smiled at her when she acknowledged my approach. Before we could exchange hellos, however, Mojito lifted one eyebrow and tilted his head toward the pool deck. *Better talk to Dad*, his expression said.

I waved to Greta, changed direction.

Mr. Mojito had his back to me. He appeared to be deep in discussion with a group of men. So much for not having to meet and greet before the exchange of vows.

The four extra-large guys were all dressed in dark suits. Weren't they hot? There was a nice breeze off the Intracoastal, but it was going to hit eighty. At least eighty. Florida in the late spring? Black won't work if you're going to be outside at a wedding reception all afternoon.

Inappropriate clothing aside, their attitudes were all wrong. Their faces were way too unfriendly for a wedding. My fiancé was yammering away, gesticulating avidly, while the others stood frowning, arms crossed.

Once I was close enough to the clot of men, I recognized my friend from Jersey. What in God's name was Fat Monkey doing there? I doubted he'd been invited to the reception. Not after the ugly debacle of his previous visit.

My groom was dressed in tan slacks and a white tuxedo shirt. He looked handsome, distinguished, and nervous as hell. It was his wedding day, so this was to be expected. But when I slid into place beside him and wrapped an arm around his waist, he flinched. Man needed to stay cool or he was not going to make it through the day's stresses.

"Hello," I said, kissing him on one smooth cheek. "Is it time to tie the knot, darling? I doubt I can wait much longer."

The other men smiled politely. But Mr. Mojito did not. The look he gave me was that of a drowning man. He grabbed on to me like a life preserver, held on with all he had. In a shaking voice, he said, "Gentlemen, I'd like you to meet my beautiful bride, Cathriona O'Hale."

The tallest man stepped forward to grasp my hands in his. He was six-three or four, slim with sea-green eyes. He reminded me of someone but I was not sure who. "Congratulations," he said. "I'm sure you'll make our boy here very happy."

Our boy?

I recognized the accent. Another friend from New Jersey. And suddenly, I knew. This was Greta's father.

Mr. Mojito introduced all of the men at once. "Darling, I want you to meet my clients, the Cantoli brothers."

Aha. The final missing puzzle piece instantly slid into place. Greta's disappearing pregnancy. The ongoing affair with Mojito. Fat Monkey's recent visit regarding my fiancé's serious financial problems. Money, debt, the Cantoli brothers.

My heart bounced up and down. This was going to be easier than I had imagined. Because Mojito was not hot for Greta, he was helping to protect his devious dad. After the pregnancy scare had passed, father must have instructed son to keep dating the unstable girl. That way, Mr. Mojito could use her as leverage. And the good son hung in there, giving his dad more time to get himself out of his mess.

Which was where I would come in. Another patsy in the grand con. Ha.

So that was that, you see. Or so he thought. Mistake, mistake. This thing was not going to go down the way Mr. Mojito expected.

The band was setting up on a makeshift stage under a billowing white tent. The caterers pushed their rolling carts of covered silver dishes down the slate path and disappeared one by one under the tent.

I grinned at the Cantoli men like the usual dizzy bride. "So glad you could join us today. Please, make yourselves at home while we get through the vows. Then we can all have some fun."

"Greta is a big admirer," her father said to me. His sharp eyes did not convey any depth of feeling. I wondered where his wife was. "I hope you'll return to school next year so she can enjoy your senior class literature seminar."

I nodded, noncommittal. But I did not expect to be there for Greta's senior year. Not if I could help it. In fact, by the time school started in the fall, I planned to be happily ensconced somewhere romantic with Greta's boyfriend.

Taking my fiancé by the upper arm, I asked the men, "Do you mind if I steal him away? It's almost time for the ceremony."

They said nothing so I led him off. We walked slowly at first, then he steered me down the lawn toward the Waterway. Sun dappled the dark blue water. Sailboats sauntered by. The view was postcard picturesque. The perfect spot for a wedding.

He said, "If you're worried that having all these people here will ruin the exchange of vows, don't. We'll be out on the boat. Nobody else will be there, just us and the kids. And the minister. It will be quite private."

Yeah, private, right.

I said, "What do you mean, minister? I thought you hired a notary?"

His arm tightened against my hand, held it fast to his side. "Why didn't you call me back last night? I was going crazy with worry. You get cold feet?"

I stopped, hugged him tight, gave him a sensual kiss. Put on a superb show for any guests who might be watching. Then I said in my sweetest voice, "Of course not, darling. It's bad luck to speak the night before the wedding. We shouldn't be together now, actually. I'm supposed to walk into the church on the arm of my father while you wait for me at the altar with stars in your eyes."

A few tears edged out. He thought they were for my dead father. They were not. A gnat had flown into my left eye at just the right moment, and me being me, I took advantage of the timing.

He reached up to gently wipe away my tears. "Poor darling. Anyway, we'll make the best of it. You're here with me now, and we're together. The minister texted ten minutes ago to say he's on his way. Let's wait on the deck for the kids, shall we?"

We linked arms and he escorted me down the dock to the boat. I sat gingerly on the edge of one of the deck chairs, perching there like a nervous bride on the edge of her marriage bed. He stood beside me. The boat rocked gently, sensuously. And there we waited.

My darling was uncharacteristically silent. Lost in his own plans for escape, absolution, everlasting happiness.

After a few minutes, I kicked off my heels. When I put my feet up, he walked around behind me and massaged my neck. We both looked out as a cigarette boat roared past.

"So that was Greta's father?" I asked softly. I didn't want my voice to carry up the lawn.

"Yes. He's a client, actually."

"Right," I said. "And we can discuss that later. After you fire the maid."

"Maid? What maid?" His phone pinged and he said, "Okay, heads up, Cath. Here they come."

25

Greta and Mojito came down the dock, followed by a short bald man in a collared suit. I slipped into my heels and stood, straightening my dress, patting my hair. Time to make this thing legal. Time to become Mrs. Mojito. Well, Mojito one. Two would have to wait.

The minister looked the part. He carried a bible and never cracked a smile. His voice was unusually high and he had a bit of a nervous tic that made him blink a lot. He had a role to play and he made it look good. We all did.

The vows were simple. Repeat after me. I do. So do I.

After Mojito handed his father the simple gold wedding band, my husband slid it on my ring finger. It fit perfectly.

Done.

He kissed me sweetly, said, "I love you." His eyes wandered past me though. They did not stay where a new husband's eyes should remain.

I too looked over at Mojito. "You too," I said. Then I kissed my new husband like I meant it.

Too bad, too bad I did not mean it. I don't think either of us had the right kind of love, not for one another. But we did have need. A temporary need. The wedding, of course, was a sham. Soon enough, the farce would come to its proper end. I knew this, and I knew my husband did as well. My advantage was that he did not know I thought the same. He did not know I knew what he had planned for me. And he had no idea what I had planned for him.

No wonder he was in over his head with the wrong people. My new husband was a player, but a lousy one. Even I could outplay the poor man.

After the minister pocketed his envelope of cash, he left. The four of us stayed on the boat for a few minutes congratulating ourselves and hugging. Mojito was stiff in my arms. Our eyes skated across one another's masked faces. Greta felt as thin as a Popsicle stick. She said to me, "You look so happy. I'm so happy for you."

She meant well, dear girl. Another person ignorant of the harsh reality of her own life.

My groom and I followed the kids up the slate walkway and across the lawn to the tent. Clusters of guests clapped as we passed by. I waved to a tight band of teachers from school standing together by the dance floor. I would have to go over there and show off my ring, act giggly and thrilled.

But first, I needed a drink. At least my thirst was not going to be a problem. It was open bar and the booze was already flowing freely.

With the men in black gone, my new husband eased into his role as consummate host and proud groom. I had to admire his acting skills, he was wholly convincing. When we danced, he stared in my eyes. He kissed me passionately out on the dance floor, again at our table between dances, and once more after we cut the triple-tiered white-on-white wedding cake.

The reception went on all afternoon. The band my husband had hired was lame, playing dumb songs from the 1960s, but they managed to get folks dancing. The high school kids turned up their noses at the goofy pop music, trooping down to the dock to smoke weed. I longed to join them, but made do with endless glasses of Cristal. I removed my shoes and danced barefoot, swirling around like this was my moment, my dream come true. I lifted a glass to each and every champagne toast. Flashed my fake diamonds and made crude jokes with the women from work. Met all my husband's guests and acted appropriately thrilled to have landed such an incredible catch.

The enraptured bridegroom and his devoted bride. Ha.

As the afternoon melted into evening, I kept an eye on Mojito. He drank a lot, danced little, hung out with the dopers, and appeared uncharacteristically sour. Greta followed him around like a starving kitten, mewling in his footsteps.

Poor baby was suffering. He wanted me, not a stepmom. Soon he would have what he wanted. What we both wanted.

This gave me enough optimistic energy to continue my bridal act until the last guests had dragged themselves out front to overtip the valet. Mojito's glum dejection underscored his strong feelings for me. My poor boy. So sad because he thought he had lost me. To his dear father.

But he had not. He would not. Because I had other plans for us.

The sunset raged orange and red. While my husband paid off the band, I joined Mojito, who had crashed by the pool. Greta slumped in a deck chair, her tight dress up around her panty line. Mojito lay beside her on a lounge chair, Ray-Bans covering his eyes.

"Not *so* bad," he said without context.

I wasn't sure what he meant but Greta laughed. Then she turned to me. "When I get married, I want a wedding just like this one." She smiled at me, her young eyes full of hope. "Fun, relaxed, and *so* romantic."

Beside her, Mojito smirked. I wanted to slap his face, then fuck him silly. But that wouldn't have been appropriate behavior for a brand-new stepmom, now would it.

When my husband joined us poolside, he had a fresh bottle of Cristal in hand and a stack of plastic wine glasses.

"Smart, using plastic glasses by the pool," I said, trying to elicit a response from Mojito. His face remained expressionless.

My husband continued in the gracious host role. "I want to thank all of you for making this important day one of the best of my life," he said as he passed out the glasses. "My beloved family." Then he popped the cork.

What could I do? After he poured me a glass, I smiled sweetly at him, keenly aware of the tragic truth in the statement he had made to us. His wife, his son, his son's lover. His son's two lovers. His wife who *was* his son's lover. I sipped at the bubbly, laughing to myself and thus realizing just how drunk I was.

Drunk enough to join the others in the swimming pool? Yes, that drunk.

My husband went first, removing his white loafers, wading out on the steps. He called to his son, who shed his morose attitude to join him in the water, both men knee deep in infinity. Greta couldn't sit this one out, she kicked off her six-inch Louboutins, padding across the deck to the steps into the shallow end. While dipping a toe in, she beckoned for me to join her. So I did.

Soon we were all giggling and gossiping about the wedding guests. This one was blind drunk, that one had his eye on so-and-so. I was laughing much too loudly at the kind of thing I generally have zero tolerance for. Was this the new me? My husband turned around and caught me by the neck, kissing me roughly, hungrily, before climbing out of the pool.

I watched him as he ambled back to the empty tent in search of more unopened bottles of champagne.

The day had been a success, I thought while trying to manage the whirlies. Now my new life would unfold. With my husband and true love, all under one roof.

"He's so into you," Greta said wistfully.

Poor naïve girl. Slurring slightly, I said, "You'll have all this too one day. A man who loves you, a beautiful home, and a good life ahead of you. Just make sure you get that MIT degree first."

She nodded. "I'm on it. I'm gonna apply for early admittance. I'm gonna apply in the fall."

Mojito was to continue his studies for another year at FBU in order to finish up his associate's degree, then he would head off to a top university. At least, that was his father's plan for his son. But not mine.

I looked at my boy, waist deep in the pool, Ray-Bans on a cord around his neck. His eyes were glazed and his mouth hung open. He was drunk. Or stoned. I had to get him away from his father. From Greta, God bless her romantic little soul. He had ambitions, energy, a brilliant mind. I fervently hoped all that would not go to waste. It would be so easy for him to follow in his father's footsteps, or to fall for some average girl who could entrap him in a suburban mundane life. This would be the ultimate tragedy. Wasn't it my job as his teacher to make sure this did not happen?

Greta eased down the steps, daring to get soaked in order to join her boyfriend. She screamed at the stupidity of her decision to wade in. Turning toward us, Mojito gave me a fast but searching look. I mouthed a pouty kiss. He shook his head, disgusted with that response, and looked away.

Greta screamed again, wading out above her hips, venturing deeper and deeper until the water was up to her Barbie doll waist. She shrieked with laughter.

I seated myself on the deck, with only my feet in the water. My husband sat down beside me, sliding a cool hand up my leg to my upper thigh and keeping it there. Possessively, as was his right.

"This is nice," he said, his voice marked by the usual tone of sincerity. "Family."

Right. But I knew the future. This happy little 'family' would not last. Because soon enough, Mojito and I would be together. It would be Mojito and me alone in our elected paradise.

A paradise the color of a hell-fire sky, but a paradise nonetheless.

PART III

THE SUMMER

26

My lawyer has suggested I provide you with a detailed and frank account of everything that occurred after the wedding celebration. I'm not about to bore you with the day-to-day tedium. But I guess I cannot avoid telling you the most sordid details. After all, I want to convince you of my need to do what I did. So let me begin by saying my new husband insisted on constant amorous exercise. This meant I had to feign passionate delight for more hours than I thought humanly possible.

Wasn't sixty too old to be oversexed in this way? No, not anymore. Thanks to the miracles of modern medicine, romping without an end in sight has become the bedroom norm for oldsters with access to the proper enhancement drugs. I am a casualty of that futuristic horror. Mr. Mojito stocked up at the local pharmacy and boisterously reassured me he had an ample supply packed for our honeymoon cruise. Which would begin as soon as Mojito and I finished with school for the year.

Needless to say, I was exhausted before we even left the dock. Based on his suffocating animal need for me, I had plenty of reason to cut the romance short. Please. Sex with an old man does not turn me on. Hours and hours of old man sex, night after night after night? My worst nightmare. There's only so long a woman can maintain the closed-eyes fantasy that her partner is forty years younger and romantically desirable.

While I finished out the final term at school, I spent as much time as I could at my condo, correcting papers and avoiding my wifely duties. Finals week flew by as I dealt with the onslaught of Wiki-ed term papers and lackluster CliffsNotes-based essays. Due to a district-enforced parental decree, I handed out unearned As to all my seniors. After that, I had to endure the annual drudgery of attending yet another graduation ceremony. Yawn. But seeing my beautiful boy dressed in royal blue cap and gown made all the suffering worthwhile.

Mojito remained distant and sullen throughout the post-nuptial/pre-honeymoon period. Greta made up for his lack of attention to me. Whenever she saw me, she reminisced dreamily about the wedding. She told me about her summer school plans (four courses at FBU), her new prep tutors (for the SATs), and a European backpacking vacation she was embarking on in July (without Mojito, thank God). With continued good humor, she threw a last-day-of-school bash at her place. I had never been, but my husband described her father's house as a modernized castle in a miniature slash pine forest. Complete with a shallow moat and a guarded drawbridge.

Nouveau mob style, anyone?

Of course, Mojito's parental units were not invited to party with the kids. So we stayed home and my lust-crazed husband tortured me with his overmedicated magic wand.

On the day we were scheduled to embark on our honeymoon, I had already endured enough sex for ten brides. I excused myself from the boudoir so I could go home to pack my travel togs. I also planned to bask joyfully in some well-deserved alone time.

I got into my car carefully. Oh, my poor body hurt. I wasn't as limber as I'd once been. I really was not built for gymnastic sex. A stairwell encounter once in a while was the most I could manage. Actually, that had been fun. As I exited the Mojitos' driveway, I dimly recalled the way I lost control that day, the ecstasy of the moment.

Sad! Only a few weeks of the wife-life and already I was beginning to forget how much I had once enjoyed sex? I shook my head. The situation was dire.

When I got home I parked in my spot, entering the building through the front doors. The lobby was empty. No sign of security. On my way up the stairs, I was tempted to do something nasty. Take off my panties and wave them above my head, perhaps. In case anyone was watching. But I was too tired to even do that.

I had yet to box up my belongings and move into the Mojitos'. If all went according to my plan, it would be unnecessary anyway. Thank God for that. The nasty maid still skulked around, since my husband said she was "part of the family." My dear husband was a menace in the bedroom. And, at any moment, the Cantoli brothers might drop by with a steel-jacketed solution to the debt argument.

The cats whined when I opened the door. The poor things were hungry, even though I'd left them plenty of food. They didn't like for me to be gone for more than a day or two.

"Sorry, guys," I said as they followed me out to the kitchen, jostling me with their pushy little bodies. "But it gets worse. Next up for you is a trip in the carriers."

I swear, Zora shook her wide head. I didn't blame her for saying no. And I understood why she would prefer to stay home and sulk. But Tina had volunteered to take in my kitties for the duration of the honeymoon. Which was kind of her, but not acceptable to the cats. They were true homebodies.

Sacked out in a lounge chair on the patio, I sipped a bloody tequila and read over the story I'd been working on. I had been fictionalizing my journal to create the semblance of a novel, wildly enhancing the truth with details from my salacious imagination. Between spikey tomato sips, I added multiple new scenes. The wedding ceremony and reception, the grueling post-wedding nights, the week of continued bedroom acrobatics. I started a draft for the chapters on the cruise to the islands. I would need to fill in the specifics later.

With a grunt of satisfaction, I set aside my laptop and removed my reading glasses. Draining the last drop of enlivened tomato juice, I felt my strength returning, my resolve solidifying. I'd put up with enough. It was time to prepare for the upcoming honeymoon tragedy. The denouement, as we say in the literary world.

Since I had hacked his computer and read his files, I was quite sure my new hubby was making plans for my demise as well. In that way, we were a perfect couple. When I stood, however, my tender areas protested, reminding me of the important ways in which we were, in actuality, so very poorly matched.

And so it was with no trepidation whatsoever that I went to the kitchen to retrieve the vial.

Let us back-step for a moment so that I may share something with you.

On a quiet Saturday several weeks earlier, I had made an emergency visit to my dentist. I complained of a striking pain in a back molar and insisted on a root canal. This had to be done before my month-long cruise to the islands. Better safe than sorry, I repeated, even after the X-rays revealed no sign of infection.

I knew my dentist, however, and he always said the patient

knows best. He was also a man who understood the kickback value in patient referrals. So refer me he did. The following Monday morning, a skilled periodontist performed an emergency root canal, showing me her sternly disapproving face much of the time, muttering into her mask about *oversensitivity* and *perfectly healthy roots*.

The pain med prescription she gave me was an extra strong one. People who suffered the way I did with no apparent cause? These special patients needed more than the usual dose prescribed for post-surgical pain. If she went easy on me, she might be answering to late-night emergency calls. And who wanted that? I told her I had trouble taking pills. Could she prescribe something that would be easier for me to swallow?

That was how I scored the vial of liquid Dilaudid tucked away on my pantry shelf. With a burst of enthusiasm, I retrieved it and poured the full contents into my trusty travel flask. I mixed in one jigger, then another, of Mezcal.

That done, I packed for the islands. The requisite lingerie. Two pairs of stretchy white shorts, a black dress, several wraparound skirts. A small pile of billowy T-shirts and blouses. Hiding my belly had proved easier than I thought. The loose clothing worked wonders and nobody seemed to notice my mysterious weight gain around the middle.

I packed books by Camus, Rilke, Ken Bruen. My iPod, ear buds. Bathing suit and flowered silk cover-up, sunblock, coconut after-sun crème. Hats with wide brims. Sandals, heels. Toiletries, makeup. Reading glasses. Phone, laptop. Mask, fins, snorkel.

Me, with snorkeling gear? Yes. Believe it or not, this Girl Scout dropout had gotten herself prepared. Right around the time I had my root canal, I signed up for an introductory diving class. After all, we had a boat. I mean, my husband owned a boat, so *I* had a boat. Therefore, it was important to get the basics down, right? I went to the YMCA out on Military Trail twice that week to learn what I would need to know in preparation for the upcoming cruise. How to put on a mask and flippers, how to breathe through a snorkel, how to dive in deep water. How to not drown.

I hated the class, it brought back all my old fears about the water. After the class was done, I still hated the water, but I knew what to do if I had to be in it. Which was soon enough going to be the case. Because even if Mr. Mojito did not want to go snorkeling, he was going to end up in the water with me.

All part of my plan.

After a long soothing bath and a second bloody tequila, I got dressed. I had to try on several shirts until I found one blowsy enough to cover my pouching belly. My condition was obvious to anyone with an observant eye. Nobody seemed to look at me like that, however, not even my amorous husband. What, they all thought I'd gone to fat? That I already sported the blubby midriff of old age?

For once, my age appeared to be working in my favor.

I decided to have one more for the road. Or the Waterway. Whatever, I mixed myself another bloody and carried it out on the balcony. I loved sitting out there. Why was I leaving? I adored the unspoiled view of clean white sand. The big blue sky full of skeeting clouds. The gorgeous teal ocean and its frothy tide. Pelicans diving for fish. Surfers riding the curling waves. How could I let go of all this beauty?

For Mojito, I reminded myself. I would be giving up my old life, even the things in it that I loved with all my twisted heart, in order to be with him. Forever.

Legs crossed Indian style, I sat and watched as Mother Nature ate her young. The sunlight dwindled and in the distance black sky moved in. Soon, the thick rain clouds dumped sheets of water on the howling ocean. Hostile waves scraped at the half-eaten shoreline. The darkness seeped toward me until I felt a few fat drops hit my head. I had to duck inside. Mother Nature could be hungry, angry and mean. I wondered what she would do to my aged husband when I handed him over.

Whatever she wanted, I imagined. Whatever she jolly well wished.

27

After I finished my drink, I cleaned out the glass and put it back in the cabinet. With great difficulty, I scooped up the cats and plunked them in their separate carriers. Zora gave me the stink eye. Pearl curled up in a frightened ball.

I cleaned out the litter box and tossed the garbage, then I walked around my condo, unplugging appliances and turning off lights. I upped the AC to eighty, then hoisted the suitcase straps over my shoulder and took a carrier in each hand. On my way out, however, I had to stop then reload after I remembered to nab a raincoat.

The day had darkened significantly and the roads, of course, were flooded. I drove slowly through the puddled rainwater, listening to the cats whine.

When I pulled into the lot for Tipsy Tina's, their noise increased. As if they knew I was dumping them off.

I parked near the entrance and turned off the car. Then I leaned over the seat and looked at the two of them. Trapped in their little boxes, they stared out at me, unblinking, their eyes glowing in the dim afternoon light. "Zora, don't be such a baby. You'll love Tina. She's going to give you lots of attention."

Actually, I had no idea if she would. I didn't think of her as a cat person. But then again, I wasn't one either. And I had two of the silly critters.

"And Pearl, you need to chill. Maybe it will do you good to be in the big world for a change. Bring you out of your furry shell."

I was justifying. I felt terrible about leaving them behind. But I wasn't about to take them on the boat.

Tina was gracious, oohing and aahing over the two cringing cats. After I set the carriers down behind the reception counter, she promised, "I'll get them out of here by six. Soon as I close up. It's busy today. Wedding party," she explained, rolling her eyes.

All three chairs were occupied by giggling girls with rollers in their hair. Pink cheeks, round faces, small white teeth. They all looked young enough to be my students. I hoped none of them was the bride-to-be. Why couldn't kids wait until they'd launched an adult life before giving it all up to get married?

I must have looked like I had fallen into a trance because my friend put one arm around my shoulder and steered me to the door. "You tell him yet?" she asked in a low voice.

I shook my head. "No. Still thinking about that number you gave me." I meant the contact information for the doctor who was discreet. *That* number. "I don't think fatherhood's what he had in mind when he asked me to be his wife."

This was true.

Tina frowned, thrusting her prominent chin. "Tough shit. He's in it for the long haul now. He'll have to take what comes."

That he would. But the haul ahead was not going to include the opportunity for him to be a new father. Not if I could help it.

I thanked her ten more times until she practically threw me out of the salon. "Go. Enjoy your honeymoon. And make the goddam decision, okay?"

I promised I would. But in so many ways, I already had.

When I drove up the pebbled drive, my husband was standing in the doorway of his manse. The rain was really coming down. Torrential. When it rained like this, there was no staying dry. By the time I ran up the front steps, I was soaked.

He took my drenched raincoat, my damp suitcase. He seemed annoyed, so I grabbed his sagging neck and laid a soggy kiss on his pursed lips. But he pulled away, scowling. "Where have you been? The weather's so bad now we'll have to delay. Probably until tomorrow." He held me by the shoulders. "You've been drinking."

Yeah, so?

I smiled, shrugged, downplaying it. "I had a bloody while I got ready for our trip. I'm a little nervous about the cruise. Since I can't swim so well, I mean."

Since I will drug you unconscious and then drown you out there in the goddam scary ocean, was what I was actually thinking. But my spouse was right, more right than he knew. I shouldn't have been drinking. I would need to stay sober for this sweet little honeymoon of ours.

His expression eased and he drew me against his chest. "I won't let anything happen to you, Cath," he said in a mushy voice.

Liar.

This is as good a time as any to tell you exactly what I'd learned by snooping on his computer. My beloved husband was, in fact, a liar. A *professional* liar. As the Jersey Monkey had warned me, Mr. Mojito was a career con man. And now I was a part of his game. A game piece he was playing, one he had been playing all along.

Like Bernie Madoff, my husband had built a Ponzi scheme hedge fund. This kind of finance is too complex for me to understand, but ten minutes of skimming documents provided me with a good idea of what it all added up to. Suffice it to say, he took dirty money from dirty people and laundered it through a complicated web of semi-legal businesses and investments. His shady investors paid him lavishly, but of course that wasn't enough for Mr. Mojito. The con man cashed in the investments willy-nilly, sending out falsified statements while spending the newly washed money on his own lifestyle. The house. The car. The boat. The chichi Boca Club.

His scam had worked for years. But when his biggest investor the Cantoli brothers wanted to retrieve all their holdings, my dear husband didn't have the funds.

Whoops.

That's where the new wife came in handy. He had lured me into his life by wooing me, convincing me of his wealth and success, his kindness and his deep love for me. The next step was to make us both disappear and have it look like an accident. So he couldn't be held accountable for his debt. Somehow, and on this I was not sure of the details, he would also collect a nice pile from an insurance policy he'd taken out on us. I didn't know how he would do this, just that he would. I'd seen the policy in his personal files as well as his accounting for its future spending. Alive, my husband was in debt, and to the wrong sort of people. Dead, there would be no more debt *and* there would be serious compensation.

As I understood it, Mojito would inherit everything. Dad would be in hiding somewhere, sans stepmom of course. He would be carrying on solo and incognito, living the life. And, although the boy would be left behind to face the angry investors, that wouldn't be an issue. After all, a kid couldn't be held accountable for the sins of the father. A decent lawyer could take care of everything. A contact person at a high-powered Palm Beach firm was listed in my husband's files.

But what about the wife? Oh, yawn. She was expendable. A pawn he would sacrifice in order to correct his past mistakes. The double insurance policy would set up Mojito. He could go to a top college and not have to worry about student debt.

I might have hated my husband for this. But how could I when I planned on sacrificing him in much the same way? I too would sacrifice him for the greater good.

The greater good being Mojito.

Stuck at home for the time being, the newlyweds made do. I changed out of my wet clothes while he prepared us a simple dinner. Then we vegged on the couch in the living room and binge watched *The Blacklist*. My husband loved that show. I think he fancied himself a real-life Raymond Reddington. The ultimate gentleman con man with a soft spot for his girl. Or was it an incestuous desire for her? That's the only aspect of the show I found of interest. The subplots were dumb, the characters trite, but the father-daughter flirt was intriguing. And, of course, I preferred any show to going upstairs for hours of gymnastic sex.

We watched six episodes, then went up to bed. The rain had stopped, and the night air was cool and still. I opened a window and stared out at the stars, the reflections bright smears in the peaceful Waterway.

In the morning, there was a loud rapid knock at the bedroom door. My husband rolled over, mumbled, "What?"

I jumped up to answer it. I expected Mojito. I hoped it would be him. We hadn't said goodbye. I wanted to at least be able to do that.

But it wasn't Mojito. It was the maid. Or whatever my husband preferred to call her. The vacuumer.

I said, "Hey. What's up?"

She glared. "Want to talk to him."

Behind me, my husband called out, "Let her in, for God's sake."

Curious, I stepped back so she could come in the room.

Mr. Mojito sat propped up against the leather headboard, his black sleeping mask around his neck. In the early morning light, his chest looked sunken, the gray hairs curly and, well, ancient looking. I headed for the bathroom to get dressed.

"On the job men. Out by the boat. They know you up here, *jefe*."

"Motherfucking cocksuckers!" my husband erupted. "Get Mojito on the phone. He knows what to do. Then go tell them I'll be down in a few minutes."

She left the room without another word. I stood there, frozen in place, while my husband jumped out of bed and hustled into the previous night's slacks. Were we in trouble? Who was it this time, the Cantolis or some other irate mobsters? Would my plan be ruined? Right when I was so close to achieving success? And what about Mojito? How deeply involved in his father's cons was he?

When my frazzled husband finally noticed me on his way out the door, standing in my nightie in the bathroom doorway, he stopped for a second. "Be ready to rock outta here, babe. We go the minute they do." He nodded to me once, then left.

This was the first time I noticed an accent. The motherfucking cocksucker had hidden it from me. But the truth was unmistakable. The man I'd married had a New Jersey accent.

Damn!

28

In an agitated daze, I threw on shorts and a top, zipped up my suitcase. Lugging it with me, I bumbled down the stairs. I needed to get a look at these visitors, I had to assess exactly what was going on.

The vacuum bitch was nowhere in sight, so I eased up to the edge of the sliding glass doors and peeked out.

The sun poured down like white gold from a giant pitcher. It splashed on everything. The water, the boat, the Popsicle-blue pool, the lush green yard. The garden was ablaze in refracted light and fresh bloom, blood red impatiens and purple snap-dragons, hot pink wax begonia and frangipani. And the roses! Bleeding from their thorny stalks in neon reds and pinks, canary yellow and pure snow white. The roses sat drinking in the morning rays like ambrosia.

Mr. Mojito stood way out on the lawn. He was noticeably smaller than the visitors, two big men in dark conservative suits. My poor husband was gesticulating and talk, talk, talking. Fifty feet away and I could smell his desperate fear.

I jogged over to the front door to check out the visitors' car.

Black Ford sedan. Tinted windows. Florida plates. Government issue? Sure looked that way.

Back by the sliders, I tried to hear what my husband was saying but the glass was too thick, the distance too great. The two men towered over him, their arms folded across their chests. They wore mirrored sunglasses, their faces solemn, unreachable. I could see the sweat stains on my husband's white shirt.

After the visitors turned away and headed off, disappearing around the side of the house, I ducked away from the glass doors. When Mr. Mojito walked in, hands running through his hair until it stood up like a clown's, I was waiting at the bottom of the stairs, suitcase in hand.

"Ready, honey?" I called out gaily. "It's such a beautiful day!"

He grunted, did not meet my eyes. "I need a shower. Can you get us some breakfast?"

What could I say? I set my bag by the sliders again and walked down the hall to the kitchen to prepare eggs and coffee. Like any wife would do in the situation.

Inside my head, the wild surf pounded at the shore, tearing the beach apart. But my hands were steady as I brewed up a pot of Starbucks Colombian and heated a slab of butter in a frying pan. Act like everything is fine, I told myself. Then kill him first before that lying fucker from Jersey gets a chance to kill you.

I broke the eggs, checking for blood spots. There were none.

After we finished my four-egg green pepper and onion omelet, toasted whole-wheat English muffins, and several cups of strong coffee, I did the dishes. "You'll do fine as the galley chef," my husband said. "I think I'll call you Skipper."

Really? Please. "No, darling. *You're* the skipper. I'm your gal Friday."

As if.

He forced a husbandly smile, but I saw through the veil of deflection into the well of his dark unbridled fear. He reeked of it. My husband was in trouble. He was in the deep shit.

Knowing this buoyed my confidence. A scared man is a distracted man. And a distracted man is a defenseless man.

I followed him to the foot of the staircase, then asked if Mojito was going to come by to bid us *bon voyage*. My husband turned, lifting one brow in surprise. "He will if we ask him to. Why?"

I shrugged, acting casual. "You don't need to talk to him before we leave?"

"We'll talk on the phone. Text. E-mail. There are plenty of ways for us to keep in touch. We'll only be gone three or four weeks. I think the boy will be fine without us."

That's exactly what I was worried about.

"Okay," I said. "You know best."

Before he went upstairs for his travel bags, my husband flashed that warm and gentle smile of his. The one that hooked you by the heart, drawing you into his devious world of make-believe love.

I fake smiled back. Two players, both playing for keeps. I had to constantly remind myself of that. I needed to stay clear-headed. Aware. One step ahead.

Within a half hour, we were off. The sky was a wide blue canvas dotted with thick daubs of white. Despite the brisk easterly wind, the June sun felt harsh on my skin. It was sure to be even more searing the farther south we traveled. I slathered myself with sunblock, then stayed under cover as much as possible. Finally, complaining of seasickness, I left *el Capitan* up on the fly bridge navigating our way out to sea. We were going to catch the Gulf Stream and ride it to our first stop: tourist trap Freeport in the heart of the Bahamas.

I wasn't really sick, but I felt lousy once ensconced in the dull box of our cabin. I closed my eyes, trying to smooth the rough patches in my mind. There were so many unanswered questions tugging at me, strands in a messy web, filaments that led off somewhere to something, I didn't know what. The loom of the Cantoli brothers. The situation with Greta. Her brief hysteria, her sudden change in life goals. Our quick wedding. The government men. The fake investments, the money laundering, the scamming, the debts. The fat insurance policy. The Caribbean vacation, the two newlyweds. Out to sea, alone on the boat.

What I needed was a drink. But I was too afraid to drink. Afraid of what cards my husband might play if I lost focus. Afraid I would somehow tip my own hand.

The sea rocked me gently like a giant cradle. I lay on the bed, reading and rereading a few lines from a paperback poetry collection. The lines were by Rilke.

It is a tremendous act of violence to begin anything. This spoke volumes.

All the soarings of my mind begin in my blood. Yes. My own blood boiled through my body like battery acid. Or maybe that was the coffee, sloshing along with the incessant rocking of the damn boat.

After an hour down below, I was crawling the cabin walls. How would I be able to take weeks of this? I wouldn't. Any sane woman would opt to kill her spouse right out of the gate and blame it on temporary insanity due to claustrophobic boredom.

I was sure it had been done before. Perhaps many times.

After a series of deep centering breaths, I left the cabin and made my way up the stairs to the deck. Looking at the turquoise ocean from my patio was delightful. Being this far out on it was terrifying. I tried not to look down as I mounted the stairs to the fly bridge. Bitter acids burned up the back of my throat.

When I said hello to my honey, he didn't look up from the computer screen. "Fuck me, Cath," my no-longer-curse-averse husband said. "There's a boat trailing us. And the motherfucker's catching up."

"What?" I joined him in front of the computer screen. But I couldn't make out what he was pointing to. Dots. Lines. So? Like so what if there was another boat out here in the Gulf Stream? Why wouldn't there be? Of course, he could've been making it up to throw me off guard. Or he might have been telling the truth. There was no way to know. So I played along. "Who is it, do you think? Pirates?"

I was joking. But his face had gone pale, the tan washed out along with his acting skills. "No. But it could be the Coast Guard. That would be the best-case scenario." His voice was flat. Like he was reciting lines.

"And what would be the worst?"

"The Cantoli brothers in a cigarette boat," he answered.

I had to agree that a mid-ocean visit from enraged thugs probably wouldn't work out for the best. Still, I wasn't sure I bought that story. Unless they thought my darling con man was trying to sail away from his debts?

I asked calmly, "So, what do we do?"

"We veer off course and circle around. Roam about like maniacs. Hope we lose them and, later, try to get ourselves back on course." He kept his eyes on the computer screen. Was he avoiding my eyes because he was lying? Or because he was telling the truth and felt embarrassed in front of his bride? "That's all I can come up with."

Really? A seasoned con and that was his most coherent plan? To spin around in circles until the problem went away?

This seemed like a ruse. I decided I wasn't worried. Whatever happened, he was still the one in trouble. Not me.

"Do what you think's best, Skipper." I put a tentative arm around his waist.

He stiffened, then relaxed into my hug. "Okay, babe. Hang on. Here goes."

He sped up until we were flying over the water. Then, with a jerk of the wheel, he spun the boat to the right and we crossed over the wake. Bouncing up, then down. Up, then down.

With a weak moan, I shuffled down the stairs to the deck. I lay on my side on a deck chair, too nauseous to move. Water sloshed up on the deck and the empty chairs slid around, crashing into one another as we hit wave after wave. Up and down, up and down. I promised myself if I got to dry land safely, I wouldn't ever leave it again. At least, not on a boat.

After a horrible span of time in which I prayed and swallowed omelet vomit with increasing difficulty, the forward motion slowed and the wave crashing stopped. When I felt able to do so, I stood and minced to the back of the boat. I looked out to sea, squinting against the rays of the sun. I didn't see anything except endless water. No other boats. I wondered if there ever had been any.

Back up on the fly bridge, my honey seemed in better spirits. His color had returned and he smiled at me. "We're okay now, babe," he said. "I'll get us back on track pretty soon, but I'll need some refueling. You want to rustle up some grub? I'm starving."

He had to be kidding. I was sideways from all the circling about and he wanted me to deal with food? And what was with the goofy slang? I had married a rich man with class, now I was out on the open ocean with a douchebag from Jersey.

When I didn't answer, he said, "How 'bout a coupla nice greasy burgers and some fries?"

I made it to the side of the boat before I lost what was left in my system from breakfast. Then I went back down the stairs to the galley to see what I could *rustle up*. It would be a miracle if I could cook food in that tight little room without puking. Again.

The refrigerator was only half size and the shelves were packed with bottles of Miller Lite. A row of bottles of cheap sangria. One bottle of inexpensive champagne. This was not my husband's usual assortment of liquid refreshments. It seemed like something a fisherman from Palatka might have on hand.

With a long sigh, I hunted through the pantry. I needed something to settle my stomach. What better choice to get me right than beer and rice crackers?

I popped a Lite and drank it nice and slow while I prepared a cheese plate with crispy crackers, black olives, and jalapeño slices. The freezer held two boxes of burger patties, a bag of shoestring potatoes, and a couple packages of white bread hamburger buns. I couldn't believe the larder. Who was this man and why did he suddenly have the desire to eat like a truck driver?

Nibbling crackers, I decided I would come back in a while to fry up the fast food. First I would serve him the snack. I grabbed another beer and hunted through the shelves for a serving platter. A green plastic tray left over from the previous owner looked like it had been stolen from a hospital cafeteria. But it would have to do. I loaded it, then carried it up the stairs to *el Capitan*.

He thanked me absentmindedly, immediately swigged his beer. Okay, so now I had my answer to a question I hadn't wanted to ask him. My husband would indeed drink and drive. This was good news for me, not so good for him.

Still, when I said I was going back down to make the burgers, he had a wide smile on his face. The poor fool thought he was getting away with something. With everything.

I didn't throw up while I fried the burger patties, but I sure felt like it. The room quickly filled with greasy smoke. Eventually, this set off the smoke alarm. I had to unscrew the battery to halt the squawking. I baked the fries in the oven and toasted two buns to a golden brown. There was no lettuce or tomato, no onion, not even a pickle. Nothing fresh and green in the galley. No fruit either. Did my devious husband plan to kill me by starving me to death? I mean, what did he think *I* was going to eat?

He was so inconsiderate. Why had I married such a lout? Next thing I knew, he'd be forcing me to watch the Yankees pummel the Marlins. Please.

With that in mind, I moved ahead with great confidence. Ducking into our cabin for a moment, I retrieved my thermos. Back in the galley, I mixed him a cocktail. Screw-top sangria with Mezcal and Dilaudid, the perfect knockout drink. I poured myself a much smaller glass of the sweet wine, hoping it would stay down. Then I carried the food tray upstairs to my man.

He sat at the helm, his eyes glued to the horizon. "Won't be long now," he said over his shoulder. He got that right. Then, noticing the tray of food, he added, "Wow, babe. That looks awesome."

Babe? Awesome? I couldn't help it. I had to say something. I handed him the glass of sangria. "You even sound younger out here at sea. I told you it would be good for you to buy *Clytemnestra.*"

He nodded, grinning like a kid. "Even ditching the pirates was fun. Got my blood pumping." He eyed me up and down. My hair was limp from the grease that flew around the galley. My skin was sunburn pink with a tinge, I was sure, of seasick green. He licked his lips. "Makes me randy for sea candy."

Barf. That had to be the perfect exit line. I couldn't bear to hear any more.

I held up my glass. "So here's to the best honeymoon ever."

We clinked, and he chugalugged like a champion.

29

By this time, you must have a good understanding of my side of the story. There I was, in a dangerous situation with a dangerous con man who had married me under false pretenses. I was seduced while he pretended to be something he was not. He was neither rich nor a gentleman. And worse, he had whisked me away from my life, from my home and my job, from the boy I loved. Plus, he'd taken out a policy on me and planned to do away with me. Fake his own death, then collect. Do you see why I had no choice in the matter?

No? You don't see it that way? Never mind, never mind. Let us go on with my miserable story.

I took over at the helm while my husband dined. Chowed down was more like it. He ate like a clam digger. What had happened to the classy man who rubbed elbows with the one percenters at his snooty private club?

Fortunately, he did pause between greedy mouthfuls to swig his medicine. *Glug glug.*

"'Long have I longed,'" I said, reciting stolen lines he had used in his own poetry. "'Farewell all things that die and fail and tire.'"

He looked at me, his lips grease smeared, his eyes blank, not comprehending. Like one of my dulled students, only decades older. I shivered.

I needed to watch what I was doing. The sea was not rough, but it wasn't calm either. I was sure I could continue to steer the tug safely after my darling husband passed out cold. But I held tight to the wheel and asked him, "How'm I doing?"

He laughed. "It's on automatic pilot, baby."

Oh.

Seconds later, he slumped lower in the captain's chair. I looked at him appraisingly. He appeared to be in a zombie daze. I had read up on the side effects of drugging someone, so I took advantage of his hypnagogic state and I asked him what I most wished to know. I was hoping to utilize the truth serum qualities that reportedly accompany a medicated brain state.

"Darling?" I queried. "Where are you from originally?"

"Newark, baby," he answered, a few leftover bun crumbs drifting from his lips to the edge of his chin, then downward. "Born and raised. Then Long Island. Side trip to Alcatraz for three. Forged checks. After that, Wall Street for finance. Worked my way up. Learned all the tricks."

There was a rather glaring gap there. How exactly did one go from prison to Wall Street? Wasn't it supposed to be the other way around? But I wanted to keep him on track with what I needed to know, so I nudged him forward with the next question.

"And why, darling heart, why did you marry me?"

He smiled, a spinnaker of drool following hamburger bun crumbs onto the front of his mint green polo shirt. "I like sex with you, babe. A lot. You Irish chicks give the best head. And now I can start over. In the Caymans. Where we have a fat fuckin' bank account."

We? My mouth fell open and a line of spit trailed down *my* chin. Did he mean Mojito was in on it? The boy was clued in to his father's devious plan to use me, then get rid of me? This seemed highly unlikely. The boy was mine. He was insane about me.

Wasn't he?

My husband was stuttering, so I leaned in to catch every word. "He kept the Cantolis at bay by romancin' the daughter. The old man likes my kid. Thinks he's gonna go far. He is. Far away from *that* fuckin' family."

My blood boiled up so that I was sure my eyes were red with it. So Mojito *was* involved. *Very* involved. Had they lied to me about the girl being pregnant? Or was that how he'd roped her in? "What about their baby?" I asked.

He shrugged, which made him topple to the side. "No, no baby," he muttered, half out of his chair.

So he'd lied about that too. What hadn't he lied about, I wondered as I stood. I used all the strength I had and heaved him back into a sitting position.

He laughed. "Oh, y'mean this?" he said as he grabbed my protruding belly, holding the extra flesh in a somewhat painful grip. "Not to worry," he mumbled. It was almost impossible to understand him. "S'floatin' in booze anyways."

What?

I reared back. Oh my god. He meant *me*. My baby. *Our* baby.

Mistake, mistake. *I* could drown the poor thing in liquor, but *he* had no right to insult it. Or me. Or what we'd made together. Or, maybe, didn't.

I pulled away, then I slapped him. I whacked him good, right across the face. He flew out of the chair, landed in a heap. And stayed there, quiet at first, then kind of snoring. What a pig.

That was enough information out of him. How dare he insult our unborn child? His child. Or maybe his grandchild. Whatever, that was low. And not gentlemanly at all. I heaved a loud snort of disgust. Then I stepped over him and went down to the stateroom to get the rest of what I would need.

It was going to be even easier than I'd imagined to say goodbye to my deceitful husband.

When I came up again on the fly bridge, snorkel gear in hand, he was no longer snoring. Maybe he hadn't even been snoring before. Maybe he'd been dying.

I nudged him with my foot. Kicked him. Lifted an arm, which fell back with a thud. Dead weight. When I prodded him with my finger, his skin felt clammy. I checked his pulse. There wasn't one. I'd squashed him like an annoying insect.

And what did I feel? I felt immense relief. And intense fear. For there I was, out at sea, alone. A poor swimmer, an inept boater. And a murderer. With a dead body onboard.

My bloodbeat jackknifed and a dull roar began in my ears. It was coming from my brain. My body tingled as I rushed to the side of the boat. Without hesitation, I heaved. So much for keeping down those few sips of sangria.

While I wiped my foul lips on my shirt sleeve, I looked out to sea. I needed a place to stop so I could get him in the water. Set up the snorkeling accident. Then drag him back onboard.

It wasn't going to be easy. But then again, it had to be better than whatever he'd had in mind for me.

And when it was all over, Mojito and I would be together. No matter what they'd been up to, the two Mojitos, my boy would have no choice. His father was dead. He was my stepson. He was not yet eighteen. He would have to stay with me.

Long have I longed.

Well, no more of that.

30

A few hours later, I spotted a small island up ahead. I'd been trying to keep the boat on a southerly route, but of course I had no idea what I was doing. However, luck was with me. Land ahoy!

The island was more like a hammock, just a spit of land covered with large black rocks and spindly trees. I dropped anchor and hefted the body by lifting it under the armpits. With much difficulty, I dragged my darling husband down the stairs to the fore deck.

After taking way too much time to inflate the life raft, I managed to get him into the rubber boat. It was difficult, but I was able to use those hidden sources of superhuman strength all wives have.

Ha.

His body felt even heavier because it was already stiffening up. Wow, that was quick.

With awkward ineptness, I paddled us over to the island, trying not to look at the water. It scared me even more than the corpse. The things a woman will do for love! This thought made me laugh to myself.

Once we hit the shallows, I climbed out of the raft. The water was warm and clear, up to the tops of my thighs. Colorful parrot fish darted between my legs. The sensation was pleasant.

I pulled the raft to shore, beaching it on the rocky sand. Then I struggled with the corpse until I was able to slide him over the side of the little boat. Sand and small stones stuck to him as I rolled him back into the sea, letting the body sink. It wasn't deep, maybe up to my knees. I kept him there for a while to make sure the salt water filled his lungs. Overhead, there wasn't a single cloud. Just hot naked sun, like a searchlight on high. I needed my sunglasses, a wide-brimmed hat, things a real Girl Scout would have had with her.

So much for proper planning. But being sunburnt and bedraggled would work in my favor. Later, when the authorities arrived.

It was twice as difficult for me to heft him back into the raft. He was rigid, his body waterlogged and bluish. Wet sand clung to his face, his clothes, and his skin was pockmarked from pebbles. I'd need to clean him up a little when we got back to *Clytemnestra*.

Paddling us back there, I was filled with a rare kind of energy. Even though I was exhausted and soaking wet, my exposed skin burning in the late afternoon sun, I felt powerful. In charge of myself, my own life. I rowed soundlessly, with smooth stroke after stroke. I felt alive in a live world.

This made me smile. I was so enjoying the feeling of my wildly alive body surrounded by raw, unspoiled nature. Alone, so alone, and yet so full of life. I laughed out loud. I must have looked like a madwoman.

Perhaps I *was* a madwoman.

After we pulled up alongside and I tied up, I found I couldn't lift him from the raft. There was just no way. I struggled for what seemed like an hour. My muscles ached, and I was so thirsty I was coughing, hacking. Finally, I gave up. I would have to leave him there and tow him behind the boat. I had no other choice.

So I left him lying in the raft and climbed back onboard.

I went straight to the galley for a drink. Would it be too crass if I opened the bottle of champagne, I wondered? I was in a cele-bratory mood, after all. But no, not wise. So I settled on beer. I popped one open, drank that baby right down. A cheap Lite beer had never tasted so good.

I returned to the raft with the snorkeling gear, which I dipped in the ocean before arranging it beside the body. I dunked a pair of my husband's swim trunks, then pulled off his wet clothes. It was a bitch to change him. I don't want to talk about how that felt, undressing him like that.

Not sure what to do with his sandy and sopping clothing, I stuffed it all in a garbage bag and added the frozen packages of beef patties as ballast. Then I tossed it overboard and watched it sink.

I grabbed a few more beers and headed up to the fly bridge. Seated in the captain's chair overlooking the calm ocean, the rubber boat with the body, the clean deck swabbed of evidence, I popped another Lite. Then I said out loud, "*Now* I'm the skipper."

I pulled up anchor, drifting along. Alone under endless blue sky on an endless blue sea. I let time pass, then I let more time go by. The little hammock I had rowed to was long gone, replaced by open water the color of Mojito's eyes.

Mojito. Poor boy was an orphan. Thank God he had me. At least he had a stepmother to look after him.

It was late in the day when I finally radioed for assistance. *Help, my husband's not breathing! He went snorkeling and now he's not breathing!*

I opened another beer while I waited for a response.

The rescue boats from Nassau were on their way, a deep-voiced dispatcher soon informed me. Wait where you are, he said. So I did, although the boat kept drifting. Would I know how to drop anchor? Nope, I was the clueless grieving wife.

While I waited for the authorities to arrive, I thought about my situation. The groveling love I still had for Mojito. The cold facts his father had shared. The senselessness of hoping for a sensual reconciliation with Mojito. He'd been part of a long con in which Greta and I had been victimized. He'd been in on it with his con man dad.

But he'd been fooled as well. I had done my share of lying. We could work things out between us, I was sure of it. Love would see us through. We could live on *Clytemnestra* for a while, retrieve the money from the account in the Caymans. We could travel the world, take our pick of places to settle down. He could surf in the choicest locations, attend a foreign university. We could raise the baby together.

I laughed out loud. My husband lay dead, his body floating on a rubber raft below me in the rocking cradle of the sea. And here I was, drinking lousy beer and making grandiose plans for myself and my stepson while chuckling like a lunatic. Perhaps I could take advantage of this temporary insanity when the ocean police arrived.

At some point, a beer bottle slid from my hand and hit the floor with a loud crack. It rolled away, crashing to the deck below, scattering shards of glass everywhere.

EPILOGUE

ONE YEAR LATER

The rest of my story has been reported extensively by the news media. The rescue, the scandal that followed. My rapid arrest. Not for culpable homicide but for plain old first-degree murder.

I guess instead of reading classic literature, I should have been watching *CSI Miami*. I would have learned that you dunk the victim in the water *before* they stop breathing. If you fail to do that, the medical examiner can tell that the victim died from something other than drowning, and he or she looks closer. Like at the contusions on his face from when I slugged him, and the Dilaudid in his bloodstream.

Duh, as the kids say.

Speaking of kids, I found it terribly disheartening to learn that Mojito had disappeared. He did not return for the funeral, the inquest, my hearing. In fact, they're not sure where he is. My lawyers tell me the Mojito family maid who was not a maid was from the Dominican Republic. She met Mr. Mojito while working as a cleaning lady on boats in the Caribbean. She'd been the boy's first babysitter, his nanny. She lived with them over the years, stayed on after the wife left, and raised him like her own son.

It was this strange woman who gave him the nickname. Not Mojito but *Mijito*. Which means *my little sweetie*.

Good for her. Maybe she guided him through some underground railroad down there in the islands, stopping only to pick up the fat pile of embezzled cash his dad left in the secret account. Maybe she led him to a magical tunnel so he could pop up in another kind of life, one where he can't be extradited back to the U.S. I don't know. But she's apparently disappeared as well. At least, that's what they tell me. When they come by to grill me some more about my relationship with Mojito.

The key word being *grill*.

The prosecution is claiming we were in cahoots. Mojito and his teacher/lover/evil muse. They insist he had to have been on the boat helping me. That I couldn't have done what I did alone. This is sexist thinking. Of course I could do what I had to do to save my own life, to protect myself from a desperate con man. Plus, to think Mojito would be involved in his father's demise is utter nonsense. Mojito would never participate in that kind of violent act. Patricide? No way. In fact, I am quite sure my true love has dismissed me from his life forever because of my actions in this regard. Even though my choices were made purely for reasons of self-defense.

Although there's no evidence to support that either. Mr. Mojito's laptop is nowhere to be found, and there appears to be no paper trail for the insurance policy he took out on us. In fact, the lawyers tell me this would not have been possible, that we weren't married long enough for such a policy to be issued.

I find this information surprising, but within the realm of possibility. This must have been part of the con too. Maybe my two-faced husband had planned to show me the phony paperwork in order to convince me we both had to disappear, leaving

Mojito with a double payout—one that did not really exist. All part of Mr. Mojito's plan to hoodwink me into running off with him, to escape his irate investors, his deep debt, his incipient arrest for fraud. And part of his plan to use me to assist with his temporary delay tactics, only to get rid of me pronto—as soon as my usefulness expired.

Mistake, mistake, my dear con man. Women are a lot smarter than men might think. Ha.

Too, too bad for them.

But try telling this to the FBI, the SEC, the DA, and all the other acronyms lined up to question me about my husband's illegal activities. I'm not going to be as helpful as they might hope. Which is, in many ways, also too bad.

And there was bad news on the pregnancy too. It turned out to be another con, this time instituted by my own body. Ascites. Ever hear of it? Medicalese for when the liver is failing and the abdominal cavity fills with the body's own fluids. The belly, therefore, was swelling from booze, not baby. Other symptoms —the nausea, the vomiting, some confused thinking perhaps, all due to a diseased liver.

So as you might imagine, that was not a happy discovery. Although, in facing my current legal circumstances, organ failure might positively influence my sentencing. No access to alcohol could help slow the process, but the dire prognosis I now face will make my term in prison shorter by default.

A good news, bad news situation if I ever heard one.

At this point, you're probably asking yourself *why*? Like, *why the teenage lover*? And, *why marry the aging father*? Even, *why this whole mess she's made of her life*?

I wish I had answers for you, but I am lacking coherent conclusions. All I can tell you is Mojito was like an eraser mark on the white pages of my life. And yet, he was also the most beautiful illustration imaginable.

You might say I became the architect of my own undoing. What had I done with the raw clay of my life anyway? Nothing, certainly nothing worthwhile. But my undoing? That was a true masterpiece.

If I am forced to pinpoint a subconscious reason for my destructive life choices, however, I am at a loss. For the sake of discussion, I will recount one story from my unremarkable youth. One brief memory that explains nothing, yet haunts me to this day.

Each summer, I was sent away to horseback riding camp by my unloving parents. Hugh stayed home, where he had the two of them all to himself while I slept in a cabin full of immature girls. The kind of giggly beasts who think having a big animal between the thighs is better than sex.

I knew better.

The summer I turned thirteen, I fell ill at Camp Burning Birch. It came upon me suddenly while I was swimming in the lake. After I went under, and stayed under for some time.

The so-called lake was more of a scum pond actually, lurking in a deep basin of pine needles under the towering evergreens of northern New Hampshire. The blue-black water was always cold, the weak sun blocked by the thick woods surrounding it. All summer long, I shivered, protested, refused to go in. They couldn't make me. My parents were paying them to warehouse me, but the staff had no say over what I did and did not do with my time at camp.

Mostly, I hung out. I smoked cigarettes with a few of the counselors-in-training. I drank sodas with Sierra, the wild lady sailing instructor. I developed crushes on the rarely seen boys across the lake at Camp Burning Elm. For sanctioned activities, I rode horses and made lame art like gods' eyes and braided rawhide key chains.

It was Sierra who talked me into taking swimming lessons.

She told me the fastest way to conquer my fear was to dive right in. I claimed I was not afraid, just warm-blooded. I was from Florida, after all, where the ocean was eighty-five degrees. But she saw through my protests and lured me into the lake with promises of sailing together to Burning Elm after dark for boy-hunting purposes.

That got me in the lake. But the dark water bit my tender skin, clung to me. It clawed at me until I learned to stay afloat.

Then one day I paddled out too far. My arms and legs grew tired and I treaded water for a while. The lapping at my face was pee warm, but my feet felt ice cold. This was unsettling, and I became disoriented. The cloudless sky surged toward me, looming, as if it might swallow me up.

I slapped around, beginning to panic, and swallowed some pond water. Soon I felt weak. Nauseous. How could I return to shore? It was so far away.

I went under. And I did not come up again. Not for a long time.

When they dragged me ashore, I wasn't breathing. The freaked-out CITs fetched the head counselor, who administered CPR. I don't remember that. I do recall vomiting up black lake water. I remember lying on a cot in the camp office, a cool cloth on my head. I don't recall the ambulance ride, or the nights I spent at the local hospital. I have a hazy memory of feeling scared and confused, sick and alone.

My parents eventually showed up to fetch me. When I cried with relief to see them, my father snapped at me. "Grow up," he said. "Haven't you caused enough trouble for one summer?"

I felt only antipathy toward him after that. My mother's chilly silence was even more hurtful. I hated her with a quiet passion that did not diminish until the day she died. The day they both died.

That's the only trauma I can fish up from the depths of my

shallow early life. Perhaps the near-death experience permanently scarred me. Maybe the trauma taught me not to trust adults. Not to count on them. Maybe it made me self-destructive. But did it pervert me? Turn me into a cougar and a cold-blooded killer?

Perhaps I died then, and something else possessed me. Something dark and soulless. Like what Mojito saw in me, and in himself.

I guess the jury will have to decide.

I will say this. Sometimes you can only possess someone by offering them destruction. Mojito was like that. So was his father. And me? Well, you know the answer to that. After all, you know me now—as well as anyone ever will.

So, dear ladies of the jury, please reflect on this sad tale of romantic love and loss. Gentlemen of the jury, please try to be kind. I am a flawed human being, a woman with a slippery self that eludes even her. All I can tell you now is this: I still love him hopelessly. I do. In the projection room of my mind, deep in the innermost wound full of unsalvable pain and despair, he is still my beautiful boy. He is in a freeze frame there, a crystalized snapshot, so tantalizingly and so miserably unattainable. As he was then at seventeen.

He's eighteen now. A man. But in my mind, my true love will always be a boy of seventeen.

Here's a surprise: Greta comes to visit me sometimes. She rarely speaks of Mojito. *Finis*, my friends. *Finis*. We mostly talk about literature. She's decided she wants to be an English professor. A women's literature major, to be specific. She's off MIT and has plans to attend Wellesley instead. I offered to write her a recommendation, but she told me she wanted to get accepted on her own merit.

She's going to be all right, that girl. She has her priorities straight now.

Please believe me when I say I once did as well. But then I met Mojito.

And now you have finished reading my sinister little memoir. You have read of my sordid plot, and theirs. You know about my deep burning love. The betrayal. The con. So you know why I am still drunk on the impossible past. I have a right to my terrible thoughts. I could have kept them to myself. Instead, I have shared openly with you my poor sad truth, insisting that you and the rest of the world know how much I loved.

And I did love. A forbidden, beautiful, passionate, and hopeless love.

Mojito, oh Mojito, drink of my youth. My heart and my reason, my loss of reason. So wrong for me. But without Mojito, my life is nothing but an empty glass.

A glass, you see. Do you see now?

THE END

ACKNOWLEDGEMENTS

One of my favorite classic novels is *Lolita*. Although the book has long horrified readers (and nonreaders who refuse to even go there), I am a fan of Vladimir Nabokov's brilliant depiction of American morals and suburban life. His sly humor in telling that famous story is dark and biting, like chocolate with chili pepper. I wondered what it would be like to read a similar story with a seductive female predator in place of Humbert Humbert.

I owe much to my writing friends for encouraging my work: Athena Sasso, Jade Bos, Michael Cantwell, Steven J. Flam, and Aggie Cousino. Gratitude to Gordon at Shoe Music Press. A special thanks to McGarvey Black for leading me to the best press for my book.

Many thanks to Bloodhound Books: Betsy and Fred, Tara Lyons and Heather Fitt, and editor Morgen Bailey.

As always, nothing would be possible without the support of my boys—who encourage my projects even when the subject matter is controversial and possibly kinda twisted.

Made in the
USA
Middletown, DE